CW00449815

~ MURDER ON ST. MARTIN ~

A Rex Graves Mystery

C.S. Challinor

Perfect Pages Literary Management, Inc.

Second Edition (previously Murder in the Raw, 2009) by permission of Midnight Ink, an imprint of Llewellyn Worldwide Ltd. Cover design by Kevin R. Brown Editing by Connie Hill 2nd Edition editing by PPLM Cover changes and formatting by Perfect Pages Literary Management, Inc., in the US.

CONTENTS

CAST OF MAIN CHARACTERS

REX GRAVES, Scots barrister and amateur sleuth
PASCAL, limo driver at La Plage d'Azur Resort
LT. LATOUR, gendarme at the local commissariat
MONSIEUR BIJOU, a property developer with hedonistic tastes
GREG HASTINGS, manager of La Plage d'Azur Resort
HELEN D'ARCY, who takes a Caribbean cruise in a hopeful pursuit of Rex Graves

GUESTS AT LA PLAGE D'AZUR RESORT

~ ~ ~ ~ ~

SABINE DURAND, the captivating French actress who disappears
VERNON POWELL, a New York entertainment lawyer married to the actress
PAUL & ELIZABETH WINSLOW, owners of the Swanmere Manor Hotel in England
BROOKLYN CHALMERS, self-made millionaire and international playboy
DR. VON MUELLER, wife **MARTINA**, and daughter

GABY from Vienna, Austria

DAVID & **TONI WEEKS**, proprietors of the French School of Cordon Bleu in London

DUKE & **PAM FARLEY**, oily Texas tycoon and his trophy wife

DICK & **PENNY IRVING**, promoters of health, fitness, and naturism, from Toronto

SEAN & **NORA O'SULLIVAN**, founders of the Coolidge Theatre in Dublin

ST. MARTIN,

FRENCH WEST INDIES

TESTIMONY OF DAVID WEEKS

It is unbelievable that Sabine Durand is dead. She was the essence of our group, the lingering perfume, if you will. Whenever I evoke St. Martin, it is always Sabine I conjure up in my memory.

I often saw her walking at dusk along the shore, always alone. Our beach cabana is the last of eight before the promontory of rocks begins on the eastern side. She would have had to climb those rocks to get to the strand of beach beyond, but she was agile enough, I suppose. In any case, there was no other access except by boat. People sometimes dock their catamarans on that side, but since you can sunbathe nude all along La Plage d'Azur, there really isn't any point in going over there, except for privacy. People, after all, pay big money to be seen in the buff at La Plage.

My wife and I have been coming to St. Martin for ten years now. You end up synchronizing your holiday with other couples. It's always the same crowd in July:

Paul and Elizabeth Winslow, Dick and Penny Irving, the O'Sullivans, the von Muellers, the Farleys ... Duke Farley has been bringing his new wife, Pam, the last couple of years, so I suppose it's not exactly the same crowd as before. Brooklyn Chalmers brought a girlfriend two years ago, but not this time around. And, of course, Vernon and Sabine. July is by far and away the best time. August is Swingers' Month and come September you run into hurricane season

I don't know whether we'll return next year. It won't be the same without Sabine, and I doubt Vernon will come back, poor fellow. He must feel dreadfully guilty. After all, he never accompanied his wife on her walks, though I think she preferred it that way. She was remote and mysterious. I think that was part of her allure. She drew people like moths to a candle. You wanted to protect her from singeing her wings sort of thing. Well, the others will say the same, I'm sure.

Sabine always wore the diaphanous white pareo on her walks. She would have taken it off before she went for a swim, of course, which would explain why part of it was found by the rocks. But she wouldn't have gone for a dip right before dinner. I don't go for the shark theory—she would have known better than to go swimming at dusk. Then again, she was never the sort of person to do what you'd expect. More likely a stalker was involved; actresses often attract that sort.

It must have been after six p.m. on Tuesday 10th when I saw her for the last time on her walk. We usually all meet at seven for drinks at The Cockatoo. My wife Toni and I sometimes escorted Sabine to the restaurant on her way back, but it was Paul Winslow's birthday, and we didn't want to be late, so we left our cabana in good time. We never saw Sabine again.

Those are my recollections of the night in question.

Signed,
David Weeks

ONE

Rex Graves rested the testimony on his knees and tilted back his seat. White ridges of clouds floated outside the airplane window, while inside the first class cabin the mutedly excited voices of vacationers arose all around him. He checked his watch: another hour before they landed at Princess Juliana International Airport. He waved over the flight attendant and ordered a Glenfiddich on the rocks before settling down to extrapolate the pertinent information from David Weeks' flowery statement.

He wondered again about the people with whom he'd be spending the next few weeks at the request of the Winslows, the new owners of the Swanmere Manor Hotel in southern England where he had solved his first case. Sabine Durand had mysteriously disappeared while they were together on their annual vacation on St. Martin, and they'd asked him to fly over, all expenses paid, to look into the matter.

Paul Winslow, who suspected foul play, had persuaded the local Gendarmerie to send over copies of the statements of all the guests present at the resort on the night Sabine went missing. The von Muellers had been at the airport meeting their daughter off an Air France flight and had not returned until late, and consequently, their statements had not been taken. The Irvings from Canada had gone on a day trip to the neighboring island of St. Barts, arriving back at the resort at some time in the evening.

Winslow had explained it was only due to the intervention of a certain Monsieur Bijou, an influential developer on the island, that the gendarmes had deigned to draw up a missing person's report at all. As it was, they had not arrived until the following morning, and the two detectives from the Police Justiciary had not taken the statements until two days later. Rex swirled the ice cubes in the bottom of his tumbler, reflecting that any evidence, including footprints, would have been compromised by the time the gendarmes arrived, and the guests would have had time to work on their alibis—assuming one or more among them was guilty.

According to Winslow, the gendarme report cited the recovery of a gold ankle bracelet, identified by the guests as having belonged to Sabine Durand, and a strip of bloody gauze, apparently from the white pareo referred to in Weeks' testimony. A pareo, Rex had discovered, was essentially a sarong. In addition, the husband's cell phone had been retrieved in the vicinity of the secluded beach.

Until Rex visited the spot and interviewed the guests himself, he couldn't begin to draw any conclusions as to what might have happened to the young actress.

"We'll be landing momentarily," the flight attendant said, relieving him of his empty glass.

The plane descended toward an ocean of shimmering blues and greens. A crowd of spectators slid into view on the sandy beach, faces uplifted as the 757 skimmed over their heads before touching down on the runway. When the plane taxied to a stop, Rex let out a sigh of relief. Fear of flying was second only to his fear of the water, and it had been with a tightness in his gut that he had said goodbye to his son in Miami after a brief stopover from Scotland.

Gathering his hand luggage, he joined the line of passengers in the aisle and inched his way to the plane exit. A breeze ruffled his short-sleeved shirt, a welcome change to the muggy heat he had left just hours before in Florida.

This'll do me just fine, he thought as he contemplated the low buildings clustered on volcanic hills overlooking the rippling expanse of the Caribbean. He imagined a pirate sloop moored in one of the bays, a Jolly Roger billowing from the topmast.

Only when he discovered his suitcase had not followed him onto the plane did his sunny mood cloud over briefly.

The clerk at the lost baggage counter handed him a pack of emergency toiletries. "If you leave the number of your hotel, we'll call when it arrives."

"I'm staying at the Plage d'Azur Resort on the French side."

"Oh, you won't be needing clothes there," the clerk assured him.

"What d'you mean?"

"It's a naturist hotel."

"A what?"

"Clothing is optional."

"Optional?"

Why had Paul Winslow not thought to mention that little detail? Did he think Rex's Scottish Presbyterian sensibilities would be offended by the prospect of public nudity?

Aye, it might have influenced my decision to come, he conceded as he made his way out of the terminal, holding on to the word "optional."

Optional meant he had a choice.

He was glad now he hadn't packed his laptop. Winslow had advised against it, saying there was one Rex could use at the resort office.

A man in the crowd held up a sign with "REX GRAVES" in bold letters. A welcoming smile cracked his walnut-brown face. He had a youthful expression and the whitest teeth Rex had ever seen, though he might have been forty. Bald-headed, it was hard to tell.

"I'm Pascal, da hotel driver."

"Pleased to meet you. How far to the resort?"

Pascal said it depended on traffic, it was at the other end of the island, and asked if Rex had a suitcase.

"It went AWOL. This is all I have." Rex held up his briefcase and carry-on. "Fortunately I have a change of clothes in this bag."

"You won't be needing dem," the driver said, taking the bag and leading Rex out the exit. "Ev'rybody go about buck naked at da resort." In the parking lot, he opened the trunk of a shiny black minivan and installed the sparse luggage.

"Mind if I sit up front with you?" Rex asked, never one to miss an opportunity to find out as much as he could about where he was going.

"Sure. It be just da two of us. No more guests be arriving now till August." The driver held open the passenger door. "Which cabana you staying at"

"Number one—with Brooklyn Chalmers."

"Real nice American gentleman. You been to Saint Martin before?" Pascal asked, hopping in beside him.

"This is my first time to the Caribbean."

"Where your accent from?"

"Scotland."

Pascal started the van. "Never had nobody from Scotland before. There be a couple from Ireland an' two couples from England. Mostly we get Americans. The Irvings come from Canada. They got piercings ev'rywhere. And I mean *ev'rywhere*."

Rex thought about this for a moment. "Ouch," he said.

"Da young lady dat went missing from da resort, she went to school in England," Pascal continued, turning onto the main road. "But she lived in Paris. Mr. Winslow tol' me you was investigating her disappearance. He say to take good care of you. So you need anything, Mr. Graves, anyting at all, you jus' holler." He grinned broadly, displaying his pearly whites.

As they passed a quarry and several car rental agencies, Pascal told Rex they were going to the northeastern part of the island. "Dis here da Dutch side; they call da island Sint Maarten. Da capital be Philipsburg, named after Cap'n John Philips, a Scotsman in da Dutch navy all da way back in the seventeen hundreds."

"A Scotsman? Very gratifying," Rex said with smug pride, feeling more at home now in the narrow streets of the suburb, where rickety second-story verandas jutted out from pastel-colored houses. Pretty girls with cornrows of beaded braids toted wicker baskets laden with tropical fruit on their hips. Rex craned his neck for a better view of the picturesque scene.

Native pedestrians assumed right of way over the small, dusty cars on the road. What few signs existed were bilingual, and he had yet to see a traffic light.

Pascal went on to tell him that Christopher Columbus discovered the island on the date of the Feast of St. Martin, sounding as though he had given the tour at least a dozen times before.

A border sign in French welcomed them to the northern half of the island. Pascal explained that this side was an overseas territory of France. Rex sincerely hoped he wouldn't be called upon to use his execrable schoolboy French during his stay. The thought of having to flounder through the intricacies of Gallic grammar while standing there starkers was the stuff of nightmares.

His worst fears materialized when, half an hour later, the minivan turned into the resort.

"*Soyez le bienvenue!*" a naked Paul Winslow greeted him from the main entrance, waving a crusty baguette in the air.

TWO

Rex shook Winslow's hand. "Good to see you again."

The first and last time Rex had seen him, at a reception held for the acquisition of the Swanmere Manor Hotel, Paul Winslow wore a dinner jacket. He had a pleasant face, with graying hair beginning to recede at the temples, and stood five foot nine in flip-flops, his pale English skin reddened to the hue of a boiled lobster. Rex made a mental note to slather on sun cream while he was here. He didn't want to end up with his skin matching his hair.

"They have a shop off reception where you can buy an assortment of French delicacies," Winslow continued in English. "This bread is delivered daily. Sorry I couldn't meet you off the plane myself, but Elizabeth took the car into Marigot. Did you see your son Campbell on your way over?"

"Aye. He's so tanned I hardly recognized him. He's spending part of the summer in Miami with his girlfriend." A rich Cuban beauty who looked like she had just stepped off a fashion runway.

The driver took Rex's baggage out of the van, and they followed him down a sandy path to a wooden cabana resembling a chalet, the first in a shallow semicircle of eight located on the beach.

"How are the renovations coming along at the Manor?" Rex asked Winslow.

"Pretty well. It was a last-minute decision to come to Saint Martin, but as Elizabeth pointed out, it'll be a while before we can get away once the hotel reopens. The contractor is a reliable fellow and we felt we could leave the work in his hands for a month."

Pascal waited for them on the porch.

"Here we are." Winslow opened the front door onto a tiled hallway. "We typically don't lock our doors. There's a safe in your bedroom for valuables, and two guards patrol the resort."

"Is there much crime on the island?"

"Theft is a problem, but none has been reported at the resort in over a year. All the same, it's a good idea to keep your mobile phone locked up. You can't use it on the premises anyway."

"Why not?"

"It's considered a breach of privacy, old fellow. Mobile phones can take photos and videos. This is a nudist resort, after all."

"Aye, I wanted to ask you about that." Rex tipped the driver and he left. "I hope euros are okay."

"Euros, dollars, it's all viable currency here." Winslow led him into the open-plan living and kitchen area where glass sliders offered a panoramic vista of powdery white sand, coconut palms, and turquoise sea. Everyone outside was naked. "You must be dying to get out of your clothes," he said

"I'm not sure I want to wander about in the altogether."

"Oh, you'll get used to it. Comes a point where it seems silly bothering with clothes. Just do what you're comfortable with."

Rex averted his eyes as the nude man bent to open the fridge door. "Brook said he left you a stock of beer in case you arrived before he got back. I told him you were a Guinness man. Would you like one?"

"Aye, thanks." The can perspired cold droplets in Rex's hand. He took a few gulps and exhaled. "That's better," he said.

Winslow helped himself to a Heineken. "I hope you'll get on all right with Brook. He's very personable, really. The other alternative would have been to have you room with Vernon, but he's still in a state of shock and probably needs his space, even though it's been a week since Sabine disappeared."

"Was he very fond of his wife?"

"Crazy about her, although there were arguments between them. She was a very beautiful woman and, naturally, Vernon got jealous over all the attention she received. Sometimes I think she provoked it."

"Provoked his jealousy?" Rex asked.

"I think she liked to see how far she could go and led men on just for the fun of it. Wouldn't surprise me if Vernon snapped that night and wanted to teach her a lesson. I'm not saying he necessarily meant to kill her."

"How long had they been married?"

"Seven years. She was a young thing of twenty-one when they wed. He's thirty years older."

"Something would have had to happen to make him snap enough to kill her after seven years." Rex crushed the can in his hand. "Do they recycle here?"

"Good God, you're a powerful chap. Lost some weight since I saw you, didn't you? Yes, there's a recycling bin outside the main building, by the Laundromat, or you can leave it for maid service." Winslow hesitated before adding, "I ought to mention that some of us believe Sabine and Brook were having an affair."

"Was Vernon aware of it?"

"Not sure, but he started acting quite frostily towards Brook. If Brook and Sabine were having it away, they were quite discreet about it."

"Any suspects other than the husband?"

Winslow examined the green bottle in his hand. "I don't want to tell tales out of school—I just want to get to the bottom of this. When Sabine disappeared, my wife thought you might be the man to help. Not to put too fine a point on it, we're all successful businessmen and professionals here, and you can understand what makes us tick. It won't be too much like having a stranger among us."

"You think it was one of the guests?"

Winslow gave a reluctant shrug. "A guard patrols the beach at night and he didn't see any non-resorters up at this end. If there was a struggle, as the blood on the pareo fragment suggests, it's more likely the assailant was a man, don't you think?"

"Possibly. Does this security guard work for the resort?"

"Yes. Another one patrols the gate and walks around the outer perimeter. They're very unobtrusive, and it gives the guests a sense of security."

Rex had noticed a man in a khaki uniform when the driver pulled up in front of reception.

"Well, I'll leave you to it," Winslow said. "This is the best time of the day for a dip. The water's warm and the sun's not too hot."

"What's the average temperature?"

"Low eighties, but the trade winds cool things off. I'll swing by at seven and take you to The Cockatoo to meet the others. David Weeks can't wait to make your acquaintance."

Rex couldn't wait to meet him either, nor any of the other suspects. "Aye, see you then, Paul. And thanks for your hospitality."

"Think nothing of it. You're not just here to work, you know." Winslow picked up his baguette from the breakfast bar and saluted him with it.

When he had left, Rex entered the bedroom where Pascal had deposited his bag and briefcase. He hung up his change of clothes in the wall closet and, upon rummaging in his bag, realized he must have foolishly packed his trunks in the missing suitcase.

Och, the heck with it, he said to himself, stripping out of his clothes.

Wrapping a white bath towel around his waist, he

drew back the mosquito screen in the living room and stepped onto the back porch.

A sandy trail led through clumps of sea grape to the water. The beach formed a two-mile crescent around the bay where a tri-catamaran and a couple of sailboats bobbed on the blue surface. Beneath lurked darker patches of seaweed. On the sand, yellow umbrellas resembling inverted sunflowers shaded nude bathers on their lounge-chairs. The concession serviced the entire beach, which was open to the public, but the sun loungers and yellow umbrellas, as Pascal had informed him, were free to resort guests.

A soft contour of hills formed a backdrop to a village of bars and boutiques at the far end of the beach. In the opposite direction, beyond La Plage d'Azur Resort and boat rental shack, lay the promontory and small sandy inlet where Sabine's ankle bracelet and pareo fragment had been found.

Satisfied that no one was paying him the least bit of attention, Rex discarded his towel on a lounge-chair by the water and waded into the shallows. The sea, warm and refreshing, washed away the strain of the day spent traveling. He swam out to an anchored sunbathing raft and, hoisting himself up the ladder, surveyed the island at the mouth of the bay and surrounding blue sea. Wondering if reef sharks ventured this close to shore, he swam back in a hurry.

At the beach, he grabbed his towel and covered himself with lightening speed. Engrossed in books and magazines and in conversation, no one so much as looked in his direction. After returning to the cabana, he showered and changed into his spare shirt and lightweight pants. He would join the others for drinks at The Cockatoo, but fat chance he'd undress for the occasion.

Seated on the patio, cold soda in hand, he perused Mrs. Weeks' statement to see how it compared to her husband's.

I last saw Sabine Durand on Tuesday, July 10. We had gone over to the Dutch side of the island for shopping—Sabine, Elizabeth Winslow, Nora O'Sullivan, and myself. Martina von Mueller did not join us on this occasion since she was meeting her daughter at the airport. The Canadian couple had left on a sightseeing trip to St. Barts early that morning. Pam Farley stayed behind at the resort for a massage and facial.

Philipsburg is a mob scene when the cruise ships dock, so we always avoid Mondays and Wednesdays. I bought a silk pareo. The Cockatoo is a nudist restaurant, but there is an unvoiced rule of etiquette that requires diners to sit on something, if only one's towel. And, of course, bringing a beach towel to dinner is hardly appropriate. The men wear wraps, which looks like they're wearing aprons, and you would never catch David in an apron at home. He says he spends enough time in one at his school of French cuisine.

Our daughter bought him a Male Chauvinist Pig—oink-oink—apron one Christmas as a joke. She was about eleven at the time. Anyway, talking of male pigs, the men ate out of Sabine's hand. She had that effect on men. The young waiters at The Cockatoo were always tripping over each other to serve her. Sabine would just laugh in her childlike way, and everyone would laugh right along with her.

Going back to the other day in Philipsburg ... I bought a Delft china spoon holder and some linen table napkins. Sabine, as I recall, treated herself to a tortoiseshell compact in the shape of a scallop. We had lunch in town, and the hotel limo picked us up at four o'clock as arranged. I went back to my cabana to rest. David and the other men from our group had gone on a scuba dive that day. They didn't get back until six. David had a touch of the sun, so I made him stay in and drink lots of water until it was time to go to The Cockatoo for Paul's forty-sixth birthday dinner. Sabine never appeared.

At ten p.m., we called the gendarmes, but they didn't arrive until the next morning as they were busy with a burglary in Grand Case. The hotel sent two guards out to the rocks. It was dark even with flashlights, but they found a phone belonging to Sabine's husband. We searched all over the resort. I can't imagine what might have happened to her.

This, I believe, is an accurate account of everything I know relating to Ms. Durand's disappearance.

Signed,

Antonia ("Toni") Weeks

Contrary to her husband's testimony, which Rex had read on the plane, Toni Weeks' voluble statement showed no emotion over the loss of a friend. Her husband owned the famous French School of Cordon Bleu in London and, according to Paul Winslow, they had known Sabine Durand before she went on the stage.

The rest of the guests' statements were in the same vein. The men tended to wax lyrical while, of the women's statements, only Elizabeth Winslow's, written in an elegant hand, indicated any distress over Sabine's disappearance. He had met Mrs. Winslow at the Swanmere Manor banquet: a tall redhead who must have been a knockout in her youth.

"Hey," declared an American male voice behind him. "Oh—sorry, didn't mean to startle you."

Twisting around in his chair, Rex saw a man in his mid-thirties—athletic build, average height—and, mercifully, wearing shorts. Dark-haired and devilishly handsome, this couldn't be other than Brooklyn. Winslow had given him thumbnail descriptions of all the guests at La Plage d'Azur Resort. Rex half stood and, introducing himself, shook hands.

The newcomer exuded an air of confidence, smoky green eyes appraising Rex with frank interest. "Brooklyn Chalmers. Everybody calls me Brook."

Did Sabine? Rex decided to defer asking him about the level of intimacy between him and the missing woman. Despite his easy manner, he was clearly not a man to be trifled with. President of the Brooklyn Trust in Manhattan, Chalmers was a self-made millionaire who had piloted himself to the island in his Malibu Piper and who raced cars professionally, with a best finish of third at the Indy 500 last year.

"Thanks for putting me up."

"No problem. Sorry I wasn't here earlier. Had to fly to Aruba. Can I get you a beer?"

"No, thanks. Must be amazing to pilot your own plane."

Brooklyn sat down with a bottle of mineral water. "I can fly out to the islands whenever I get the time, without the hassle of major airports. We have a branch office in the Bahamas. Once out of New York, I set the plane on autopilot and take a nap. Next thing I know, I'm there."

Rex couldn't imagine anything scarier. "I understand you're something of a risk-taker."

Dusk descended early here, without the spectacle of a leisurely Florida sunset, he noted. Brooklyn lit the citronella candle on the patio table.

"I couldn't have gotten where I am today without taking risks. I was born in Brooklyn—hence my name—but grew up in a tenement slum in Baltimore. My stepdad worked in a factory. I painted houses through college. By the time I was twenty-one, I owned my boss's business and my first home—a modest one, but with its own four walls and a small yard. I bought one house a year after that, rented or flipped them, and then got into investment in a big way."

"Paul Winslow sent me a brief bio of you. It's very impressive."

Brooklyn proffered a disarming piratical smile. "Sorry if I sounded a bit fierce just now. I didn't want you to think I was a playboy with an inherited trust fund."

"Why would I think that?"

His host shrugged expansively. "If Paul gave you my business credentials, I'm sure he mentioned a few other things as well."

"There was mention of a special closeness between you and Sabine Durand," Rex ventured.

Brooklyn's strong profile turned toward the silhouetted palm trees. "We went horseback riding together. There's a small ranch behind the resort next to the Butterfly Farm. They kept an English saddle for her. She always rode Dancer. I'd take Rocky, the big stallion. We went riding most mornings, just the two of us, usually at Galion Beach. We'd remove the saddles and ride into the sea to cool off the horses. I know there was talk. People assumed because we were younger than the rest of the group—except for Dick and Penny Irving—that something was going on between us, but if there was I would never say anything anyway." Brooklyn sighed impatiently. "Anyway, it's all bull. After our ride Tuesday morning, we went our separate ways. I didn't see her again after that."

"When you were with her that morning, did she act as though everything was normal, or did she seem upset?"

"She seemed fine. We talked about going into Marigot that Saturday for the parade. It was her idea originally. We all discussed it at dinner the night before she disappeared, which would have been July ninth. Sabine, being French, wanted to celebrate the storming of the Bastille. Shame she never lived to enjoy it." Brooklyn's hand on the table tightened into a fist.

"Have you a photo of her?"

"You've never seen her?"

"I'm not really into the theatre, and if I ever saw a

picture of her somewhere, I've forgotten. But I'm sure Paul Winslow has some for me."

"She started getting into movies." Brooklyn got up from his chair and returned with a couple of snapshots. Holding one photo up to the porch light, Rex saw a young woman leaning against the withers of a horse, long copper hair flowing about her shoulders, a secretive smile dimpling her delicate face. Svelte in an open-necked shirt and jodhpurs, she could have been an advertisement for a lily-based English perfume. Goosebumps crept up his arms, and for a brief moment, he fell under her spell.

"Intoxicating, isn't she?" Brooklyn said.

"Interesting you should describe her that way. I was just thinking of a perfume ad." Rex lifted the second photo to the light. This one showed more of her face—almond-shaped eyes, a dusting of golden freckles across a finely chiseled nose. Her skin seemed almost translucent, her rosebud mouth a touch petulant.

"I've known a lot of spectacular women," Brooklyn said. "Most of them I've forgotten, but you never forget a woman like Sabine."

Rex handed back the photos, almost with reverence. "Aye. It's almost fitting that something mysterious became of her."

"It's mysterious alright," Brooklyn said in a voice gravelly with emotion. "I won't ever rest until I find out what happened out there by the rocks."

THREE

At seven that evening, the Winslows accompanied Rex and Brooklyn to The Cockatoo Restaurant, located just west of the resort. Chinese lanterns swung in the palm trees, lighting their way along the beach. The bay glimmered dark and unfathomable. Ever since Rex could remember, he'd mistrusted water he couldn't see through to the bottom.

Elizabeth, regal in bearing, in spite of breasts that were beginning to sag, wore a flame-colored pareo knotted at her hip. Her husband had donned a wrap. When they reached the deck of the restaurant, Rex saw that the rest of the guests were dressed in similar attire. Despite the nude torsos, he decided to keep his shirt on as he couldn't conceive of sitting down to dinner bare-chested.

"Rex Graves, QC, from Edinburgh," Paul Winslow announced to the group seated at the large outdoor table strewn with an assortment of drinks.

A plump teenage girl fed pistachios to a snowy white cockatoo perched on the wooden balustrade.

"What is QC?" she asked with a slight Germanic accent.

"Queen's Counsel. Mr. Graves is a barrister appointed by the queen of England."

"We're called advocates in Scotland," Rex explained to the girl.

Winslow began introducing the guests. "Age before beauty," he said, putting a hand on the shoulder of a Kirk Douglas lookalike of military bearing. "Vernon Powell."

Rex shook his hand. This was Sabine Durand's husband. Hard to imagine the delicate beauty wed to this wooden marionette.

"Herr Doktor von Mueller," Winslow then informed him.

"*Nein, nein!*" the bespectacled doctor objected affably. "Max. *Und* may I present my wife Martina *und* daughter Gaby."

The wife and daughter, flaxen-haired and Rubenesque, smiled in fixed beatitude. The von Muellers were not suspects, Rex recalled; they had been in Philipsburg the night of Sabine's disappearance.

"My good friends David and Toni Weeks," Winslow said, continuing the introductions. "Our new chef at Swanmere Manor is a graduate of David's school of French cuisine."

Rex extended his hand, studying the couple whose statements seemed to divulge so much about them. David Weeks, slight in frame like Paul Winslow, and with the legs of a stick insect, had a noticeably weak chin. His wife, Toni, more solidly built, appealed to the eye with her exotic dark looks.

"Duke Farley," boomed a broad-shouldered Texan, without waiting for Winslow to introduce him. "And my wife Pam."

"Enchanted," Rex replied, inclining his head politely at the couple seated at the far side of the table, and attempting not to ogle Pam's bosom, which was the largest he had ever seen while still managing to defy the law of gravity. She reminded him of the full-blown roses he had seen cascading from the walls of a chateau in the Rhône Valley at the peak of their bloom.

"Dick and Penny Irving from Toronto," a bodybuilder said, pursuing the self-introductions.

His wife didn't look like she carried a spare gram of fat either, her arms toned to perfection.

Paul Winslow hastened to make the last introduction. "Sean and Nora O'Sullivan from Dublin, owners of the Coolidge Theatre."

"Pleased to meet you," the elderly man said in a cultivated Irish brogue, his mischievous features reminding Rex of a leprechaun.

"Likewise," his petite, gray-haired wife added. "Come and sit down." She indicated a seat by her husband.

The Winslows took the vacant chairs by David and Toni Weeks, while Brooklyn squeezed in next to the teenager Gaby.

"What's everyone drinking?" Paul Winslow asked, beckoning a server.

"You should try a Hemingway," Weeks told Rex.

"A magical drink," Sean O'Sullivan chimed in. "Ice-cold coconut water, fresh lime, Gordon's gin, and a dash of bitters."

"I'll try it."

"Good man." The flushed Irishman looked as though he might have had one too many magical drinks already. He draped an arm around the back of Rex's chair. "A sad errand brings you, sure," he lamented. "We'll drink a toast and pray you can solve the mystery of Sabine Durand, God bless her sweet heart."

"I read your sworn statement...," Rex began.

"I had a wee tipple that afternoon, so my memory of events is blurred, I regret to say. But I shall never forget her."

"What was she like?"

"Ah, she was never afraid to try anything. She was Penny's scuba partner, but sometimes we dove together. What was I saying, Nora?" he asked his wife. "Oh, yes. Sabine grew up with horses. The clearest vision I have of the girl is her galloping down the beach, her light auburn hair and the horse's mane streaming in the breeze. One time we bathed in the sea off the moonlit beach. Ah, Sabine inspired me to write poetry. She was my Maud Gonne."

Nora sighed with impatience. "Just ignore him," she told Rex with a quick look at Vernon sitting silently at the far end of the table.

The waiter served Rex's cocktail. He took a sip, appreciating the clean taste of the gin, the sharpness of lime, and bite from the Angostura, all sweetened by coconut.

"What's the verdict, Counsellor? The Irishman asked, an unlit cigarette wedged in his minuscule mouth.

"Most refreshing."

By and by, the gin began to go to Rex's head, and he was glad when someone mentioned ordering food. A server handed him a menu, and he opted for a plate of melon and prosciutto, followed by grilled lemon-pepper chicken. Winslow suggested wine, but Rex opted for beer.

"Lucky you were able to get away at such short notice," David Weeks addressed him from across the table.

"The courts are in summer recess, so it was no problem."

"Hope we're not keeping you from your family," Nora O'Sullivan said.

"My son's attending university in Florida, so I took the opportunity of visiting him in Miami on the way here."

"And is there a Mrs. Graves?" the bosomy Pam Farley asked.

"My wife died five years ago."

Silence chilled the conversation, quickly filled by a few guests voicing their commiserations. Vernon Powell seemed to see Rex for the first time. A glance of sympathy passed between them.

"We must all come here Saturday," Toni Weeks said in a transparent effort to lighten the mood. "Saturday is open mike night at The Cockatoo. It's a lot of fun."

"Is this restaurant owned by the resort?" Rex

asked.

"Yes, but it's open to the public, as you can see. The Cockatoo is our usual port of call for dinner. The band starts at eight."

"There's a nightclub called Boo-Boo-Jam at the far end of the beach," drawled the balding, sandy-haired Texan. "Great for kebabs and island music. It's frequented by locals—the air is thick with dope. Sabine caused a sensation. That gal was a very sexy dancer."

Another lull broke the convivial chatter. The waiter appeared to clear away the appetizers. Rex sat back in his chair and contemplated Pam Farley in the wake of her husband's stark compliment about Sabine. Pam was younger than Duke, but not young enough to be a trophy wife still, though she tried hard to project the illusion. Rex wondered if she had felt threatened by Sabine—if any of the women had.

The closest in age was Penny Irving, another unusually attractive young woman, but whereas the photos portrayed Sabine as fragile and slim almost to the point of anorexia, Penny exuded fitness and health. Winslow had mentioned that she and her husband owned the Body Beautiful chain of health spas across Canada. Rex noticed they had each selected the leanest items on the menu.

He skipped Martina and Gaby von Mueller in his review, since they had an alibi for when Sabine went missing. Nora O'Sullivan, it seemed, had decided to age gracefully and let the gray in her hair show. With her alabaster Irish complexion and cornflower blue eyes, the effect was not unbecoming.

While Elizabeth Winslow recounted an anecdote about her trip to the hairdresser in Marigot that day, Rex took the opportunity to pass the handsome redhead under his scrutiny, guessing her to be in her late forties. Seated beside her, Toni Weeks also retained a noble beauty. According to Paul Winslow, her mother had been a distant relative of the emir of Kuwait and had married an Englishman.

"Our daughters are the same age," Toni told Rex, indicating Martina von Mueller. "Jasmin and Gaby get together each July at La Plage. Jasmin will be here next week. She's spending a fortnight in Nice with her French pen pal."

"*Und* Gaby had Latin school this summer," Martina added in heavily accented English. "She arrived a week ago."

"Latin school?" Rex inquired.

"Where we speak Latin," Gaby replied. "I want to study law, so Latin is helpful." The girl's English was much better than her mother's.

"Rex is a criminal lawyer," Toni told Gaby. "Isn't that what you want to do?"

Rex wanted to get back to the subject of Latin school. "*Num Latine ibi cotidie loqueris,*" he asked. Do you speak Latin every day there?"

"*Cotidie et omni tempore.*" All day, every day.

"That's amazing. And they say Latin is a dead language."

"So useful to have a background in Latin for medicine also," the Austrian doctor remarked.

"Well, I'd be happy to chat with you in Latin while

I'm here," Rex told Gaby, who appeared pleased by the attention.

"So, Rex," Weeks said. "Are you going to be getting into our naturist culture?"

"Och, I dinna know about that," Rex stumbled in his embarrassment, his Scots accent thickening in proportion to the alcohol he drank. "Not much occasion to go about wi' no clothes on back home."

"Is it true that it rains all the time in Scotland?" Brooklyn asked. "I played golf in Saint Andrews once and it pissed down every day."

"Aye, just aboot."

"Just like Ireland," Nora said.

"Well, don't be shy, old fellow. We'll let you keep your sporran on."

The table erupted into laughter at David Weeks' comment.

"What's a sporran?" Gaby asked.

"It's a Scottish fanny-pack," said Brooklyn. "Worn the other way round."

The guests laughed uproariously again. The second course arrived, filling the air with an aroma of savory ribs and spicy seafood. Rex attacked his grilled chicken and rice with gusto.

"Grand Case, the neighboring town, is the gastronomic capital of the Caribbean," Dick Irving, the Canadian, told him, addressing him for the first time since their introduction. "There are about thirty restaurants packed along the main boulevard."

"The town also has several cute stores and kitschy little churches," his wife Penny said.

"I passed by there on the way to the resort."

"You must have taken the Marigot route from the airport."

"Aye. The driver was verra informative," Rex added, slipping deeper into his Scots accent. "It was like having my own personal tour guide. Is Pascal the limo driver too?"

"Yes," said Paul Winslow, "but if there's a scheduling conflict, Greg Hastings, the manager, sometimes drives. A few of us rent jeeps, but cars get broken into so often on the island we prefer to be chauffeured whenever possible."

"Who owns the resort?"

"Monsieur Bijou," Brooklyn replied. "He has another hotel and a new club in Marigot, but lately he's gotten into residential projects. He just opened a luxury condominium complex up the coast."

"Marina del Mar," Paul Winslow said. "He's got fingers in several pies. It's thanks to him the police finally pulled their thumbs out and decided to look into Sabine's disappearance."

"Truth is, we've gotten nowhere in a week," Duke Farley exploded. "She couldn't have just vanished into thin air."

The guests looked expectantly at Rex, who cleared his throat. "Aye, well I'll see what I can do, starting first thing in the morning, but I cannot make any promises."

Solving the case of the missing actress might prove to be a challenge. An island in the Caribbean was an ideal place to commit the perfect crime, he reflected. If your could pitch a body far enough into the sea, you could hope the sharks would get to it before the police did. And one week had already gone by.

FOUR

The next morning, Rex set out with Paul Winslow for the promontory where Sabine Durand's trail had ended. He was relieved to see that Paul had donned tennis shorts for the expedition. Dick and Penny Irving, the couple from Toronto, were just returning from an early jog along the shore, bodies replete with artful tattoos and rings in painful places.

The presence of such athleticism made Rex momentarily consider liposuction on his love handles. Luckily, the imperfections of his body were concealed in court by a black robe, but he decided then and there to go on a diet, if only for health reasons.

"Ideal specimens of the human anatomy," Winslow remarked of the Irvings as they ran by with a wave to them. "Puts one to shame, doesn't it?"

"You're in pretty good shape."

"Nowhere near those two, but then I'm too lazy. I suppose they have to be good advertisements for their health spa chain. Vernon works hard at it too. Wouldn't go with the image of an aggressive New York entertainment attorney to be covered in flab."

"Was he in the military?"

"Served in Vietnam, I believe."

"That explains his upright posture and stern demeanor."

"Well, he hasn't much to be happy about with Sabine gone—unless, of course, he had something to do with it. But he never was much of a live wire to begin with."

They approached the boat rental shack, which had not yet opened for the day, and continued to the rocky promontory rising in their path and gradually sloping into the water.

"Watch yourself on the rocks," Paul warned. "They'll be slippery."

They walked out over the wrinkled wet sand to a low part of the jetty and climbed over to the strip of shore on the other side. Without any wind, there was not enough swell to break on the rocks out at sea.

"Today will be a scorcher," Winslow commented absentmindedly, staring out to the ocean as though it held the answer to Sabine's disappearance. "I can't bear to think what happened to her."

"I cannot understand why she would come out here," Rex said, looking about him. "Especially after dark."

Broken shells and bottles littered the windward part of the island. Scrub grew on the far side, adding to the desolate appearance. A rugged cliff blocked direct access inland, providing a cove hidden from view.

"I always think the water looks forbidding at

night," Winslow murmured.

We bathed in the sea off the moonlit beach.

The poetic sound of Sean O'Sullivan's words had taken root in Rex's mind for some reason.

"It's still grey this time of morning," Winslow remarked. "Makes me wonder what's lurking beneath."

"That's why I don't like the water." Rex scoured the narrow shore, but knew the chances of finding anything of interest were remote. Too many people had traipsed over the sand, not to mention the tide flowing in at regular intervals.

"This is where the gendarmes found her ankle bracelet." Winslow pointed to a spot above the waterline midway along the outcrop pf rocks.

"What about the bloodied scrap of material?"

"Up there where you're standing. It was caught on a piece of driftwood. The blood matched Sabine's. She had a rare blood type, so there can be little doubt it was hers."

"Who did the testing?"

"Vernon found a lab in Philipsburg. The police wouldn't pay for it. They combed the beach and questioned everyone at the resort, but they refuse to pursue the inquiry until a body is found. They did give us a swatch for the testing, though it took a bit of arm-twisting on our part."

"What did you match the blood with?"

"Max von Mueller performed cosmetic surgery on Sabine five years ago. He called his clinic in Vienna and compared the findings with his records. The blood type was a positive match."

"He's a cosmetic surgeon?"

"One of the best in Europe."

Rex found it surprising that the doctor with the round face and protruding belly was an aesthetic surgeon. He looked more like a psychiatrist or pediatrician.

They headed back toward the resort, where the beach attendants were putting up the yellow umbrellas.

Shielding his eyes from the sun, Rex pointed to the island in the mouth of the bay. "What's out there?"

"Just piles of shells and a couple of half-sunken wrecks. You can snorkel across."

"What about sharks?"

"Mostly blacknose and reef sharks. A big barracuda may skim the sand alongside you. He's just curious. Barracuda won't bite humans in clear water unless you're wearing something shiny or swimming in a school of fish. Then they might strike by mistake, same as a shark."

"What about swimming on the other side, beyond the promontory?"

"I wouldn't go out there unless you're a good swimmer. There's a strong undertow. Looked calm enough this morning, but the waters around the island can get quite rough, which limits visibility for diving."

"Do you dive?"

"Occasionally. Brook's my scuba partner. Penny and Sabine used to pair up. We'd go on shark dives where you feed them and they swim around your legs."

Rex shuddered. "You'd never catch me doing that."

"It does take nerve."

"I worry about my son surfing in Florida."

"Shark attacks are pretty rare," Winslow consoled him, unsuccessfully.

After agreeing to get together later in the day, they diverged in front of the cabanas. As Rex entered his living room, Brooklyn was just leaving, dressed in a lightweight suit.

"I left a couple of croissants in the oven for you and some coffee in the pot."

"Thanks. Off to town?"

"I have a meeting in Philipsburg. Catch you later."

Rex took his breakfast to the patio table where the previous day's *Daily Mail* was anchored by a conch shell in case of a sudden gust. Ordinarily, he took exception to the *tsk-tsk* style of the *Daily Mail*, but today he viewed it as a friend from home and eagerly turned to the Sudoku puzzle, which he completed in eight minutes flat. He wished the mystery of the missing actress were as easy to solve.

The full sun on the bay gave the effect of a blue mica mosaic. It looked inviting now, beckoning him for a swim. He prepared for the beach, his concession being to wear a white towel about his waist as though partaking of the Turkish baths. He didn't feel comfortable conducting an investigation in his birthday suit, although the public nakedness of others bothered him less than he would have thought.

"The Pillsbury Dough Boy," Duke Farley joked as

Rex's pasty-white bulk passed him on the way to the beach. The Texan said it with a pleasant laugh, and Rex didn't take offense.

"You should've seen me before I got to Miami."

Farley, in nothing but flip-flops, advised him not to forget the sunscreen. "You don't wanna get fried."

Rex assured him he wouldn't and went to find an unclaimed umbrella. The slabs of flesh on the lounge-chairs arranged along the beach reminded him of bodies at a morgue—except that the women had not gone so far as to discard their jewelry. Mrs. Winslow wore a heavy gold necklace in a Greek key pattern design that must get uncomfortably hot in the sun.

Sabine's ankle bracelet had been found beyond the outcrop of rocks. Rex pondered the significance of that. The blood on the torn strip of pareo, discovered in the same location, had proved to belong to her too. Something had happened out there. But what?

The absence of a body was not necessarily a bar to a murder charge, at least not in English law. St. Martin, part of the Department of Guadeloupe, was subject to French law. What he needed to ascertain was whether Sabine Durand had been murdered and who had killed her. The French authorities could take it from there.

Spotting a vacant sun lounger next to Pam Farley, he asked if he might ask a few questions.

Pam flashed him a toothy smile. "Go right ahead," she said in a welcoming Southern twang. Winslow had told him not to be taken in by her dazzling blonde looks. She had graduated *magna cum laude* from an Ivy League college and been clever enough to snag an oil and cattle tycoon.

Rex perched on the chair. “Your statement pretty much fits with the others. What I wanted to ask you was about Sabine herself.”

“What about her?” Pam settled more comfortably on her saffron-colored towel.

Like the other women he had seen *au naturel,* she was shaved to within an inch of her life. He concentrated instead on the attractively proportioned features of her face.

“Your personal recollections, how she behaved the last time you saw her, that sort of thing.”

“The last time I saw her was a week ago Tuesday at Happy Hour. We were at l’Apéritif, that tiki bar over there. It must have been around eleven a.m. We were drinking piña coladas—the usual crowd, except for the Irvings who’d gone to Saint Barts for the day. There’s not much to see on that island, so we declined their invitation to join them. After drinks, the von Muellers went to pick up their daughter from the airport and stayed on the Dutch side for dinner. Sabine, Toni, Nora, and Elizabeth went into Philipsburg for lunch. I’d booked a session at the resort spa at three so didn’t go with them.”

“And then?”

“After my massage and facial, I stayed in my cabana to wash and set my hair, and didn’t see my friends, all but Sabine, until dinner. I can’t remember exactly what time Duke got back from his dive, but he was already showered and changed when I was through getting ready.”

"How did Sabine seem that day?"

"Much the same as usual. I mean, when you talked to her, you always wondered if she was listening to a word you said. Her aquamarine eyes would just drift away and then, just when you thought you'd lost her, she would smile vaguely and say something apt." She waved to a bronzed couple at the water's edge.

"You weren't exactly close?" Rex prompted, drawing her attention back to him.

Pam inspected her immaculate manicure. "This is the third year I've been coming to the Plage d'Azur and I can't say I ever figured her out. Sabine was private about her past life. I believe she came from a well-to-do family of bankers in France, but fell out with her mother and had not seen her parents in years. In any case, that's what she told me. I think she was close to her father, and that may explain her air of tragedy. Unless that too was an act."

"What do you mean by that?"

"I thought her a bit of an actress, even outside of work. She was my least favorite woman friend of the group, to tell the truth—which, of course, I'm bound to do." Pam beamed him another brilliant smile. "You are, after all, investigating her disappearance in a semi-official capacity. Still," she added, "I couldn't help but admire her, just as you would have to admire a Lalique statuette."

It was becoming apparent to Rex that Sabine did not have many fans among the female guests. He wondered what other reactions he might receive. Across the beach he could make out a tall form reclining in a lounge-chair beneath an umbrella, a bejeweled right hand clasping a tall drink, the straw hat bobbing as the owner chatted to a neighbor.

"Is that Elizabeth Winslow?"

Pam squinted. "Yes. She's talking to Nora."

"I'll go and bother them now. Your husband will be wanting his chair."

"Duke went to play racquet ball with Vernon. They play every morning. As the oldest men in the group they have to work harder to stay in shape."

"You all look so fit, I'm beginning to get a complex."

"You look just fine to me for a man your size," Pam complimented him with a seductive smile.

Covering his embarrassment with a polite cough, Rex took his leave of the Southern belle and, adjusting the towel securely around his waist, proceeded to Mrs, Winslow's spot on the sand, greeting several guests on the way.

The night before, he had asked them to please confine themselves to the resort for the next few days for interviews and, for the most part, they had complied with civility, expressing themselves anxious to find out what had befallen the young French actress. Brooklyn had pleaded business appointments, but had promised to make himself available whenever possible. None had provable alibis other than the von Muellers and possibly the Irvings, whose itineraries he would have to verify.

According to David Weeks' testimony, Sabine was last seen just after six, which was close to the time the male members of the group returned from their diving excursion. No one began looking for Sabine until ten that night. A window of four hours existed during which time she vanished. If a guest had killed her, there was only one hour of opportunity before they all met up at The Cockatoo for Paul Winslow's birthday dinner at seven.

Rex hoped that under constant surveillance the perpetrator might give himself or herself away by making that incriminating slip that everyone did sooner or later. Possible, too, that the body might be washed ashore during that time. Or what was left of it.

FIVE

"Good Morning," Elizabeth Winslow greeted Rex behind a huge pair of designer sunglasses. "Are you going to try and cultivate a tan?"

"I cannot spend ten minutes in the sun without turning pink."

"Nor can I with my Irish complexion," Nora said from the lounge-chair alongside Elizabeth's.

"I was a sun-worshipper when I was younger," Elizabeth confided. "Now I'm paying for it." She had the fragile skin of a natural redhead. In broad daylight, the heavy gold jewelry around her neck could not hide the sun spots and premature wrinkling on her chest. "Won't you have a drink?" she asked. "The waiter will be along in a minute."

"It's still a bit early for me."

"Oh, we don't have rules here," Elizabeth said in her well-bred English voice. "Besides, alcohol is so cheap out here it's criminal not to take advantage."

Nora relinquished her spot beside Elizabeth. "I'm going to do my laps. Rex, you're welcome to use my chair for twenty minutes."

He duly slipped into the lounger beneath the shade of the yellow umbrella. A parade of nudists strolled along the beach while couples and families frolicked in the sea. If his starchy Scottish colleagues could only see him now...

"So," Elizabeth began. "We dragged you halfway across the Caribbean to look into our friend's disappearance. What do you think now that you're here?"

"It's a bit too soon to say."

"Forgive my impatience. You only arrived yesterday afternoon, after all."

"I take it you were close to Sabine Durand?"

"We met ten years ago when she came from Paris to work at David Weeks's restaurant. That was before he opened his cookery school. David and Toni had a small flat in Kensington back then, so Sabine lodged with us. Paul and I became quite attached to her. We married late and have no children of our own."

"And you've kept in contact with her ever since."

"We didn't see so much of her when she became involved in the theatre. The hours of rehearsal were grueling and she toured a lot. But she dropped us a line here and there, and I saved all the programmes and newspaper articles for my scrapbook."

"What do you, personally, think became of her, Mrs. Winslow?"

"Elizabeth—please." She removed her sunglasses, revealing green eyes glassy with tears. "It's not easy to say this," she said, "but I'm going to anyway. I'm certain her husband is involved. When I heard she was going to marry a much older man, I was, to say the least, concerned. Sabine was such a romantic creature. I couldn't see what attraction she could feel for a hard-nosed New York lawyer, however rich he might be. But I suppose she felt he could further her career."

Rex privately acknowledged that the husband was the most logical suspect. His cell phone had been found by the rocks. Paul Winslow had pointed the finger at Vernon too, citing his jealousy, but without concrete evidence, murder would be hard to prove. Sabine might simply have borrowed his phone.

"Have you seen the police report?" Elizabeth asked.

"Not yet. I only know what your husband told me and what I read in the statements sent to me in Edinburgh. Did Sabine ever discuss her marriage with you?"

Elizabeth nodded, studying the sunglasses in her hand. "About a week ago I noticed a nasty bruise on her arm, and when I asked her about it, she laughed it off saying she'd fallen from a horse. I must have looked sceptical because after a while her eyes sort of misted up, and she told me she had fought with Vernon and that he'd grabbed her arm in a rage."

"Did she say what they were fighting about?"

"No, but I suspect it was over Brooklyn Chalmers." Elizabeth put her sunglasses back on. "Sabine never admitted to an affair but, if you ask me, they were much more suited to one another. Brooklyn has youth and vitality, a passion for life. Vernon is so … wooden."

Rex knew he would have to elicit precise details

from Vernon Powell as to his whereabouts at the time his wife vanished. He felt his heart hardening against the man. Rex couldn't abide the idea of violence against women, and Sabine seemed such a delicate creature, quite incapable of defending herself.

He watched Nora O'Sullivan perform a vigorous crawl back to shore and then wade out of the water, shaking her short gray hair like a wet dog. Rex got up and handed her the fluffy yellow towel as she approached.

"Ah, I feel fine after my swim. You should go in, Elizabeth. The water's lovely."

"I think I will." Elizabeth took an inflatable raft with her.

Nora spread her towel across her friend's wooden lounge-chair and lay down. "I suppose you'll be wanting to question me now."

"Only if convenient," Rex said, sitting back down.

"Ask away, I have nothing to hide. I didn't want to talk in front of Elizabeth because she was fond of the girl. You may find my impressions rather different."

"Well, let's start with what you wrote in your statement. You went with Elizabeth, Sabine, and Toni Weeks to Philipsburg last Tuesday and didn't see Sabine again after you all arrived back at the resort about four-thirty, is that right?"

"It is. The last I saw of her was when she was getting out of the limo. She said she was going to reception to check her messages, and I said I'd see her later at Paul's birthday dinner. When Sean and I got to the restaurant, everyone was there except her."

"Vernon was there too?"

"No, I was forgetting. He arrived after us. He said he'd waited for his wife at their cabana until the last moment and then decided she must have gone straight to The Cockatoo from her walk."

"What was his reaction when he saw she wasn't at the restaurant?"

"He seemed calm enough, maybe a bit icy—as though he might be cross that she was late for Paul's party."

"And your husband was with you since what time?"

"Six-ish. I was in the bath, but I heard him come in. The men had been scuba diving."

"Did Sabine seem in good spirits when you were in Philipsburg?"

"That she did. She seemed excited about the upcoming parade. Of course, had she been alive during the Storming of the Bastille, she would hardly have been on the side of the rabble. But Sabine had her whims, and we all thought it was a charming idea."

"Did she mention whether she was expecting news of any kind when she left to pick up her messages?"

"I don't think so. As you know, the cabanas don't have phones, so it's quite usual for guests to go to the main building to see if anyone's tried to make contact."

"Why don't the cabanas have land lines?"

"It's considered obtrusive. And I must say, I don't miss having one when I'm here. The idea is to get away from it all."

Rex mentally added a visit to reception to his list of things to do. Perhaps someone had left a message for a rendezvous with Sabine. "What if an urgent message came through?" he asked Nora. "How would it reach you?"

"A member of the resort staff would deliver a note. That's what happened with the von Muellers. Gaby missed her connection and called La Plage to let her parents know she'd be on a later flight." Nora rummaged in her beach bag and drew out a comb. "Any messages to do with Sabine's acting work go to Vernon, since he acts as her manager." She said this with some vexation.

"You don't approve?"

"Ah, well, it's water under the bridge now, but a few years ago Sabine was supposed to play the lead role at our theatre in Dublin. When she was offered a part in a Broadway production, Vernon finagled her out of her contract with us, and the play went bust. We couldn't get another crowd-drawing actress to fill the role in time. Sabine was ambitious. She'd been trying to get into film. She felt the lure of Hollywood and no doubt thought exposure on Broadway would help."

"Was she extremely talented?" Rex asked.

"She had stage presence," Nora conceded. "How that would have translated onto screen, I can't say. I suppose, at twenty-eight, she decided it was now or never. You can cover a multitude of sins under stage makeup and lighting, but the camera isn't so forgiving. She probably thought she could always return to the stage later."

"And your impressions of Sabine Durand as a person?" Rex asked as Nora applied suntan lotion to her face with the aid of a tortoiseshell compact similar to the one described in Toni Weeks' statement.

"It would not surprise me if Sabine styled herself after a heroine in a romantic novel. One that was will-o'-the-wisp."

"What do you think happened to her."

Nora Shrugged. "She knew a lot of men. Any of them could have killed her out of jealousy."

Rex watched as she dropped the compact back in her beach bag. Did you get that item here?" he asked. "I'd like to get one for a friend."

"In Philipsburg. I'll try to remember which shop and let you know."

At that moment, Elizabeth returned with her raft. "Hope I didn't come back too soon," she said looking from one to the other as she patted herself down with her yellow resort towel.

Rex gave up his seat. "Your timing is perfect. I have a few errands to run."

"I was thinking," Elizabeth said. "If you're still here at the end of the month, there's a Full Moon Party in Grand Case on the thirtieth. You can see the stars for miles around."

"'Tis true enough," Nora chirped in. "And even more during a New Moon. There's no better place for stargazing than in the Caribbean, away from all the artificial light and pollution of big cities."

Rex said he would attend if he could, secretly wishing he had a special someone to stargaze with him. He wondered what the night skies looked like in bombed out Iraq, where his girlfriend was involved in humanitarian work restoring schools and bringing mobile water purification plants to war-displaced residents. He'd not had real news from her in two months, no inkling as to when she might be back in the UK. Fearing she might have been kidnapped by terrorists, he had contacted the British Embassy in Baghdad before leaving on his trip, requesting information about insurgent activity in the region, but no recent abductions had been reported.

Securing the towel tightly about his middle, Rex thanked the two women for their time and made his way to the resort's main building, a larger chalet than the eight beach residences, with steps leading up to the wooden porch.

"Anything for Rex Graves?" he asked at the desk. His mother was under strict instructions to call if news came from Moira.

The female clerk searched in the first pigeonhole and handed him a postcard of an orange sunset bleeding into the ocean, postmarked Puerto Rico. It was from Helen d'Arcy, whom he'd met over Christmas at Swanmere Manor in Sussex, since which time they had kept loosely in contact. With an anticipatory smile, he read the few lines.

> *Wish you were here! Really!! I went ahead and booked my passage on the Sun-Fun Cruise Line. Will dock at St. Martin on the 23rd of July. Meet me off the Olympia at 11 for lunch? Love, Helen*

How the devil was he supposed to contact her at sea? With difficulty. But that was the point, he supposed.; she was giving him little choice. He'd been noncommittal about her proposed visit to St. Martin when she suggested it. Not that he didn't want to see her—he did—but he felt conflicted by the situation with Moira and the fact he had only one week to try and solve the Sabine Durand case.

All the same, he couldn't prevent Helen from spending her summer wherever she chose, and clearly she wanted to spend a small part of it with him. He wondered if he'd be able to resist her this time in such an idyllic and seductive setting.

"I don't suppose my suitcase arrived?"

The young desk clerk shook her head in apology. "*Désolée*. Anything else I can help you with?"

"Perhaps… Did you happen to be on duty last Tuesday afternoon?"

She nodded.

"Do you remember Ms. Durand coming in and asking for her messages?"

The clerk frowned in concentration. "I think so, yes. Do you know what happened to her? It is terrible!"

"I was hoping you might help me. I'm assisting the gendarmes in their investigation." This was a stretch, since he had not yet made his acquaintance with the French police—an oversight he aimed to rectify immediately after lunch.

"Generally she received many letters, and occasionally phone messages from a chiropractor's office."

The clerk turned to the mailbox for #2 and extracted a few items. "Monsieur Powell has been picking up the important post."

"I'm heading back that way. I can take those." Rex held out his hand, brooking no protest.

As he left the lobby, he flipped through the envelopes and messages. One, dated just over a week ago, was marked for Sabine's attention. It was from a Dr. Sganarelle's office confirming an appointment.

Vernon Powell did not answer when Rex knocked. At Brook's cabana, he changed into his one set of spare clothes and went to find Paul Winslow.

"I'm going to join my wife for lunch at The Cockatoo. Why don't you join us?"

Rex declined, saying he was off to the Gendarmerie in Grand Case and could he borrow Paul's Jeep?

"Of course, dear man. Just remember they drive on the wrong side of the road here. And don't leave anything inside the Jeep as it may get vandalized." Winslow threw him the keys, and Rex took off for the neighboring town, maneuvering around potholes that heavy rains had gutted into craters and gullies.

He couldn't imagine why this long dirt stretch wasn't better maintained by the resort, and by the ranch and butterfly farm that it serviced. No wonder the guests rented Jeeps.

Once on the main road, another hazard awaited: a gigantic herd of bleating goats. He slowed to a stop while they trotted and plodded across the asphalt to the grassy hills on the other side. Cars began forming a line behind him before he was finally able to move again.

The coast road that circled into Grand Case gave a bird's-eye view of the tiki bars and souvenir huts along La Plage d'Azur. A couple of windsurfers skated in zigzag patterns across the bay. A sailboat made for the island, gliding through the blue waves.

He passed a large salt pond and turned into a street bisecting the coastal town's main boulevard, finding a parking space in front of one of many bar-restaurants by the beach. He selected a bistro from where he could watch over Winslow's jeep, and ordered a coffee and a toasted ham and cheese sandwich.

"Oooh ay le commissariat?" he asked the server when he had finished lunch, his guttural Scots tongue never having mastered the nuances of French pronunciation.

"*Par là-bas*," the man said pointing down the street. "*Rue de Hollande*."

Rex decided to walk to the police station since there were limited opportunities for parking in this part of town. Beyond the stop sign at the intersection, a two-story colonial-style building displayed the French tricolor flag, the word "GENDARMERIE" painted across its pitted stone facade. He mounted the steps and found the door locked. A glance at his watch confirmed it was past the hour for lunch. Perhaps the police took naps, per the European French custom, he thought crossly.

As he turned away, a gendarme exited a house on the other side of the street, straightening his blue uniform.

"Poovee-voo m'aider?" Rex gamely asked as the man approached. He was almost as tall as Rex, but thin as the proverbial beanpole.

"Bien-sûr. Lieutenant Pierre Latour à votre service." The gendarme gave a slight bow.

Despite the officer's assurances of help, Rex could swear he detected a smirk on his face. "Je suis Monsieur Graves. Parlez-voo anglez?"

"Oh, moi, l'anglais, vous savez... Alors, euh, what, er, is passing?"

Apparently, Latour's English was no better than Rex's French.

"I have come about Sabine Durand's disappearance."

The gendarme twiddled his mustache. "We come and search ze beach, ask many questions." A Gallic shrug of the shoulders.

"I'm aware of all that. I wondered if I might see the report."

"And your, euh, connection with ze case?"

"I'm here at the request of Monsieur Bijou."

Upon mention of the name, the officer snapped to attention. "We look all over ze island," he insisted. "We go to ze hotels and make sure ze young lady has not boarded a plane or a ferry." He held out his hands as if to indicate there was nothing else to be done. "But come. I show you ze report."

Unlocking the front door to the station house, he led Rex into a feebly lit lobby and asked him to wait on one of the wooden benches against the wall while a copy of the report was made. A few minutes later, Latour returned with two typed sheets stapled together. As Rex scanned the report, he came across several French words he did not recognize.

"*Requins?*" he asked.

The officer formed an upright triangle with his hands and slowly slid them sideways, humming the ominous theme from Jaws.

"Sharks?"

Latour nodded. "*Ah, oui, monsieur. Évidemment.*"

"Merci," Rex said. "I'll call if I have any questions."

As he turned to leave, the gendarme wished him *bonne chance.*

"How did it go?" Paul Winslow asked when Rex dropped off the Jeep in front of his cabana.

"I met with Lieutenant Latour. He was not all that cooperative."

"I didn't expect he would be. We were getting nowhere. When after a few days we realized no ransom demand was coming—Sabine's husband and parents being so rich—we began to think something even more sinister than a kidnapping had happened. That's why we sent for you."

Rex waved the papers in his hand. "I did get a copy of the missing person report. It's in French."

"Elizabeth can help you with that. She lived in Paris for a number of years."

"From what I gather, the police are blaming sharks."

"Well, it's the most facile explanation and absolves them from getting off their froggy *derrières* and doing something about it."

"They did send out a plane, apparently."

"It was probably a training exercise the navy has to perform at regular intervals." Winslow clapped the shirt on Rex's sunburned back, making him wince. "We're relying on you, old chap. What next?"

"I'd like to talk to the Austrian doctor."

"He's on the beach with his wife and daughter."

When Rex returned to his cabana to change, he was ecstatic to see his suitcase waiting inside the door. He undressed and triumphantly pulled on his Bermuda trunks, purchased in Miami. Then, with sunscreen, notepad and pen in hand, he headed toward the beach where he easily spotted the rotund von Mueller family.

The bespectacled doctor greeted him warmly, his blonde wife and daughter smiling at Rex before wading into the crystal-clear shallows hand in hand. He asked the doctor for a quick word.

The doctor gestured for him to sit down on one of a trio of lounge-chairs draped with yellow towels. "Please, proceed with your questions."

"First of all, I understand you've known Sabine Durand for five years."

"*Ja*. First in a professional capacity. Then we met again here on Saint Martin. I never forget a face I have worked on!"

"Did you do much work on her face?" Rex doubted science could fashion a face so naturally perfect as hers.

The doctor gave a dismissive wave of the hand. "A

little bump on her nose—I remove it. *Und* I erase a scar on her temple from a riding accident in Fontainebleau when she was a child. Other than these simple procedures, there was not much room for improvement. Her bone structure was *perfekt!*"

"Paul told me you were able to match the blood on the bit of pareo found on the beach with her blood type on file at your clinic."

"That too was easy. Sabine had a very rare blood type"

"How rare?"

"Type A Kp(b-)."

Rex's puzzlement must have shown. It sounded like an algebraic equation.

"Other than the major ABO blood groups, there are more than two hundred minor groups," the doctor explained. "About one in a thousand people inherit a rare type, *und* this particular type is extremely rare and belongs only to Caucasians."

"So there can be little doubt it was hers?"

Von Mueller resolutely shook his head.

"Doctor, in your opinion, did Ms. Durand seem like someone who might have drowned herself?"

"A thousand times no! Sabine had so much to live for. But yet she may have drowned accidentally."

"I'm not buying that theory. Sabine knew these waters." Rex gazed pensively toward the promontory.

Von Mueller followed his gaze. "Perhaps she hit her head on a rock when diving off? Or she fell? But no. Her body would have been found if she was that close to shore. There was no trace of sea water on the bloody strip of material." The doctor lifted his round pink shoulders in frustration. "Where is the rest of her pareo?"

Rex recognized the validity of the doctor's words. Short of burying a body in the sand, there was nowhere else to dispose of it, or any sizable evidence, unless by boat. A sheer cliff at the back of the promontory curving into the sea cut off the beach at the far side. And the barrier of jagged rocks would have made it difficult to carry a body across without being seen, since the resort stood barely a mile away. At nighttime, such a feat would have been almost impossible.

"She might have been strangled," Rex hypothesized. "Bare-handed or with the rest of the pareo. That would account for there not being more blood at the spot where the material was found. If that's the case, her attacker is less likely to be a woman, unless she's exceptionally fit and strong."

"There was perhaps some sort of struggle," the doctor agreed. "Sabine's broken ankle bracelet was found closer to the water. That might be where she drew her last breath. *Und* then she was dragged into the water and left to the hungry sharks."

Rex shuddered at the vision conjured up by a feeding frenzy of black-finned man-eaters. He glanced at the kindly doctor sitting in the adjacent lounge-chair. Impossible to imagine him doing anything other than healing people and improving their looks. But he had to be thorough. "Just for the record," Rex said, "and not because I consider you or your family as suspects in any way: What time did your daughter's flight get in last Tuesday?"

"Five o'clock. Then we went to The Créole House in Philipsburg for dinner. Gaby was hungry. She says she never has enough to eat on the plane."

Gaby could afford to miss a snack or two, Rex thought, immediately chiding himself; it wasn't as though he could talk. He surveyed the spare tire bulging over the waist of his Bermudas and resolved to lose it by the end of his trip. Salad, grilled meat and fish, he promised himself. No beer.

"We returned to our cabana at eight-fifteen or so. We didn't go out again," von Mueller said in answer to Rex's next question. "We helped Gaby unpack *und* then we all went to bed."

That left Vernon Powell, Paul Winslow, David Weeks, Sean O'Sullivan, and Duke Farley of the male guests, who had all gone diving on July 10. And where had Brooklyn Chalmers been again?

A phone conversation with the captain of the Ocean Explorer later that afternoon confirmed that the dive boat had dropped the men back off down the beach by the village just before six, although only Toni Weeks had been able to pinpoint the time of her husband's arrival at their cabana: 6 p.m. And Nora O'Sullivan, who'd more vaguely placed Sean's return as being around that hour. The other wives had been busy preparing for Paul's party. The Irvings, who had been on a day excursion to St. Barts, had missed the dinner at The Cockatoo, as had the von Muellers.

As Rex returned to the beach from the main building, he wondered if anything more might be gleaned from the police report. He would ask Mrs. Winslow to translate it. He saw her, cocktail in hand, in the spot she had occupied that morning, contemplating the cover of *People Magazine*, which featured a photograph of Sabine Durand's unforgettable face along with the caption, "Into Thin Air."

SIX

Half an hour before sunset, Rex went back alone to the promontory he had visited that morning with Paul Winslow. Weeks had seen Sabine Durand heading toward this point at just after six, giving her ample time to return before it grew dark.

As it so happened, Rex saw the Weeks strolling toward the resort. They stopped when they drew level with him.

"Are you going to the crime scene?" Toni asked.

"I wanted to get a feel for the place when it's dark."

"Night falls like a curtain here. Don't get stranded."

"I brought a flashlight."

"We'll see you back at the resort," David said. "Swing by for a drink at The Cockatoo."

"Will do." Rex, impatient to be on his way, walked on toward the outline of rocks rising before him.

From the most prominent boulder, he surveyed the darkening expanse of sea. He imagined Sabine standing there as he was now, her white pareo billowing in the breeze. What had she been thinking in those last few moments? Was someone waiting for her behind the rocks? Someone she knew? Is that why she hadn't screamed? If she had, someone might have heard. Any incriminating footprints would have been washed over by the tide or else trampled on before the police got there.

David Weeks' cabana stood at the near end of the row. He was the only person to admit having seen her on her walk, but anyone who knew her routine could have hidden on the beach until she arrived. There had been a quarter moon that night, according to several statements. At around ten o'clock, the security guards had flashed their lights over the beach looking for a body, but it was not until the next morning when the gendarmes searched the area that the ankle bracelet and scrap of pareo were found. These were the last physical traces of her. The caption from *People Magazine* played through his mind: *Into Thin Air*.

"Where are you, Sabine?" he asked the falling darkness.

Silence echoed from the looming cliffs and empty sea, followed by the mocking cry of seagulls. Clambering back down the rocks, he turned toward the resort, buoyed by the prospect of a cold beer or stout. Just one, he assured himself, recalling his resolution to drop a few extra pounds.

At The Cockatoo, he found most of the resort guests in their pareos and wraps gathered at one end of the bar. Sean O'Sullivan sat by himself, staring into the bottom of his tumbler. "*Me oul shagogsha*," he greeted Rex.

Rex took the stool beside him and ordered a Guinness.

"A man of taste," the Irishman approved. His hands shook as he touched his lighter to his cigarette.

A white-shirted bartender gave him the evil eye, even though the restaurant was open to the outdoors on two sides and no one was dining yet.

"You saw Latour from the Gendarmerie today," O'Sullivan said, studiously ignoring the bartender.

"News travels fast."

"That it does. And I suppose you're none the wiser for your visit."

"What makes you say that?"

"This whole investigation is full of crock. They know full well what happened to Sabine, but they're not saying."

"Who, exactly, is 'they'?"

"The gendarmes, the whole lot o' them."

"What do they know?"

The Irishman touched his snub nose. "Ask that cute-hoor Bijou."

"I'm hoping to see him tomorrow. What can you tell me?"

O'Sullivan cast a conspiratorial look about him. "There's been a string of missing women on the island. All beautiful, all white."

"I'm listening."

"Bijou has sponsored various recreational projects on Saint Martin: kiddie playgrounds, botanical parks, golf courses. His luxury residential project is doing a lot to enhance the French side, boosting the economy and attracting a posh class of tourist and part-time resident. He pretty much has the authorities in his pocket. He's as good as royalty here, that he is."

"What has this to do with missing women?"

"I heard he started out with seedy strip clubs in Amsterdam, and that he may have run prostitution rings before that. Young women were found strangled, and linked to his name, one way or t'other." O'Sullivan signaled to the bartender for another drink and laid two fingers on his glass.

The bartender poured a double shot of whiskey. Rex thought it just as well the Irishman had only to stumble to the sixth cabana down the beach later.

"*Bijou* is just a nickname—'Jewel' in French," he continued as the bartender moved away to serve another customer. "The murders in Amsterdam were called the Jewel Killings because semi-precious stones were found in the girls' navels. His real name is Coenraad van Bijhooven. Two years ago, a girl was found bound and gagged in a cellar on Saint Martin, dead for over a week. At least one other female body was found stripped and strangled around that time. Now, I ask you, is that not a striking coincidence?"

"Was anyone arrested?"

"Some petty criminals were brought in for questioning, for form's sake. Unlikely any of them would have left a ruby or sapphire behind, d'you think?" O'Sullivan blew a puff of cigarette smoke into the ceiling, where, a safe distance away, the white cockatoo preened its feathers on a trapeze.

"Did Bijou's name come up?"

"One rag on the island dug up some dirt and rehashed the Amsterdam murders. Our Mr. Bijou sued the pants off them. Never another word was mentioned. But he's a vicious, hedonistic shite."

"You've met him?

"Once was enough. His eyes are as cold and hard as the concrete he entombs his victims in."

"Someone could be trying to frame him," Rex said. Or else the story was a fantastical figment of the Irishman's imagination.

O'Sullivan sagged in his chair. "Sure," he said, dispiritedly gazing into his whiskey. *Where are you, Sabine?* Rex imagined him asking the dregs, just as he himself had addressed the darkness just minutes ago. And where, for that matter, was his wife, Nora?

After a prolonged silence, he decided to leave Sean O'Sullivan to his drink-induced demons. Squeezing him on the shoulder, he got up off his stool. "Catch you later," he said.

"Tooraloo."

Rex joined the rest of the group, who were discussing Vernon Powell. Sabine's husband, it seemed, was keeping to his cabana and refusing to answer the door. According to his neighbor, Paul Winslow, maid service had been unable to get in all day. "If he doesn't surface tomorrow," Winslow announced, "we'd better get management to open up."

"I don't think we need worry he topped himself," David Weeks said. "When we passed his cabana on our way here, we heard Broadway hits playing at top volume."

"We should leave him be," Toni advised. "Let him work it out of his system."

"Work what out of his system?" Elizabeth Winslow demanded. "We don't know if he's grieving or gloating."

"Really, Elizabeth," her husband chided ineffectually.

"Don't be such a hypocrite," she returned. "You know he did it."

Rex thought he should try to defuse the situation. "I'll go and see Vernon first thing tomorrow."

"About time," Duke Farley muttered. "He's the one with all the answers."

"Why d'you say that?" Rex asked.

"It's obvious he knows more than he's letting on," the Texan responded belligerently. "That's why he's avoiding us."

"Brooklyn Chalmers isn't around much either," Rex pointed out.

"Too right," the Canadian, Dick Irving, said, looking like a less hairy version of Tarzan in his short wrap. "He and Sabine were tight."

"Pretty lady!" a voice chirped.

Rex glanced up toward the rafters where a yellow-breasted macaw trailing blue tail feathers, wrapped its talons around a second trapeze.

"This place is a veritable aviary," Rex commented. "How many birds are there?"

Penny Irving, lithe and sultry in a red silk pareo knotted at the hip, threw it a cashew, which the macaw adroitly caught in its hooked beak. "Four, all in the parrot family. This is Long John. He was Sabine's favorite."

"Pretty lady!"

"He says that every time he hears her name."

"He misses her," Winslow said. "O'Sullivan's already in his cups, I see," he murmured to Rex, with a sideways look down the bar. "What was he rambling on about?"

"It seems he has a conspiracy theory regarding Ms. Durand's disappearance."

"Don't tell me. Monsieur Bijou is a sadistic serial killer, but the police are two cowardly to do anything about it."

"In a nutshell."

"Poor old sod. His mind's shot. He has the shakes, you know. Suffers from cirrhosis of the liver."

"Why is he still drinking?"

"Can't give it up. Nora put him in rehab but he managed to sneak out to the local pub. He's incorrigible."

Rex chuckled. "An incorrigible Irishman. Fancy that. So there's no truth to this story of his?"

"What do you think?"

"It does seem a wee bit far-fetched," Rex conceded. "All the same, I'll have my colleague in London do a background check on Mr. Bijou—see what comes up. What can you tell me about him?"

"He's very respected on the island. He's given the French side a certain *cachet*. His private marina community is attracting big money. And he's creating a night life to rival the Dutch side. You really must meet him."

"I intend to. What's his nationality? Dutch?"

Winslow looked puzzled. "I really can't say. He speaks perfect English and French, but now you mention it, I don't think he's either. You'll find him very cosmopolitan. Remind me to give you his number later. He's not an easy man to pin down."

"The island's not that big."

"Twenty-one square miles on the French side, sixteen on the Dutch," Winslow informed him.

"What are you drinking?" the Texan asked Rex.

"Just mineral water for now, thank you. I got a lot of sun today." And he needed to keep a clear head. The Sabine Durand case was proving to be more complex and layered than he could have imagined, and he must focus. It would be too easy to be distracted by cocktails and cockatoos, and sparkling blue Caribbean Sea.

"A Perrier over here," Duke Farley boomed across the bar. "Didn't mean to sound off about Vernon earlier," he told Rex. "I just want to put a lid on this business and get on with my vacation. If Vernon killed the gal, he needs to fess up and get it off his chest."

"I understand," Rex said. "But he's not the only suspect."

"Did you read my statement?"

"Of course."

"I never was much good at writing essays. That's why I went into oil and cattle. 'But here goes nothing,' I thought at the time. I felt I should describe that scene at our ranch when Vernon and Sabine came to visit last year. Things got pretty ugly."

"So I read."

In his statement, Duke had gone into detail about an argument between the couple over a young stable hand at his Silver Springs Ranch in Texas. The upshot was that Vernon had slapped Sabine across the face, leaving an ugly welt that prevented her from making public appearances for two weeks.

Rex had thought about the effort the police must have gone to in order to have the pages of Duke Farley's statement translated, written as they were in Texan vernacular—but judging by Rex's earlier meeting with Lieutenant Latour, he now doubted that the Gendarmerie had gone to the trouble of making certified translations.

"Ah, here comes my lovely wife," Duke exclaimed, removing the fat unlit cigar from his mouth.

Pam, her bosom visibly preceding her, sashayed over to the bar in a gold pareo spangled with silver hibiscus flowers.

"What you drinking, honey? I was just talking to Rex about the time Vernon and Sabine came to stay at the ranch."

"Highly embarrassing for everybody," Pam told Rex. "Sabine had her face on ice for two days. Fortunately, the paparazzi never got wind of it. Our staff is very discreet and our nearest neighbors live five miles away. We had to turn down invitations and tell people Sabine had come down with an ear infection."

Certainly, Vernon's alleged aggression toward his wife did nothing to endear him to Rex, but he needed to remain objective. "What happened about the stable boy?" he asked. Pam.

"Jason? Why, nothing. He wasn't to blame. He just happens to be real cute, and caught Sabine's eye. He was saddling her horse one morning, and they were laughing and maybe flirting just a little, but it got on Vernon's last nerve. He dragged her inside the house and backhanded her. I could hear the blow clear across the hall. When I got to her, she was clinging to the newel post. Not crying—I guess the shock was too great at that point. I sat her down with me on the stairs. Vernon, well, he just stared, like he couldn't believe what he'd done. Then he marched off out the door, muttering, 'She darn well asked for it.'"

"Pam called me," Duke growled, "thinking he might go after Jason. I told the boy to lay low for the rest of their visit."

"I felt bad for Sabine," said his wife, "but she really brought it upon herself. You don't wave a red flag at a bull."

"That gal had spirit alright!" Duke drawled in admiration. "She was more woman than most guys could handle."

Pam's baby blue eyes blazed her husband with a contemptuous look. Rex thought she was probably more woman than most husbands could ever wish for, but some men were never satisfied. The night had lost its glamour, the guests looked jaded, tensions ran high. Even the band sounded flat. Rex decided to call it a night and make a fresh start on the case in the morning.

SEVEN

Bright and early the next morning, Rex made his way to the main building, thinking of Helen's arrival a few days from now. And then he thought of Moira in Iraq, and felt a twinge of guilt. He told himself Helen was just a friend, a very good friend. And Paul Winslow had told him to enjoy himself while he was on the island. All the same, things were becoming a bit complicated in every direction.

"Nothing for you today, monsieur," said the front desk clerk who had been on duty the previous day and whose name tag revealed her name to be Danielle.

"Do you have the times of ferries to Saint Barts departing from Oyster Pond?" he asked.

She handed him a schedule. The ferry left for St. Barts, twenty kilometers away, at nine in the morning, returning from Gustavia Harbour at five p.m. and docking back at St. Martin approximately forty-five minutes later. He asked how long the drive was to Oyster Pond and was told it was not more than twenty-five to thirty minutes. That would get Dick and Penny

Irving back to the resort at around 6:20, factoring in disembarkation, and yet they had not joined the other guests at The Cockatoo at seven o'clock. Rex made a written note of all this and asked to use the phone.

Danielle showed him into a small office at the back of reception where he had made the call to the dive boat captain the day before. He now phoned the ferry company at Oyster Pond to check that the Canadians had indeed been on the passenger list that Tuesday, and was informed the catamaran had returned on time and the couple had been on it.

"Monsieur Graves," Danielle addressed him from the front desk as he exited the office. "Lieutenant Latour from the Gendarmerie in Grand Case is on the phone for you." She passed him the receiver.

"Rex Graves."

"*Pierre Latour. Nous venons de recevoir des nouvelles.*"

"News? Regarding Sabine Durand?" Rex asked hopefully.

"*Exactement*. Ze rest of her pareo was picked up early this morning by a fishing boat near Ilet Pinel?"

"Where is that?"

Latour proceeded to tell him in Frenchified English that Ilet Pinel was an island ten miles north of the resort. The fishermen had heard on the news the previous week that the actress disappeared from the beach, leaving behind a piece of her white pareo, and one of them called the Gendarmerie, Monsieur Bijou having offered a reward for information. "We get a lot of crazy calls," Latour lamented, "but zis one, it is as zey say."

Bless Monsieur Bijou, Rex thought. "So it's a match?"

"Match?"

"One moment, please." Rex turned to the desk clerk. "What is the word in French for when something matches something else?"

"La même, pareille."

"Thank you." Speaking into the phone again, he asked Latour if the larger fragment of material was *pareille* to the one originally found.

Latour said it appeared so. He'd had it sent to the *laboratoire*. The pareo had a part missing almost *identique* in shape to the torn item found on the beach. It also had a label from Tahiti. One of the resort guests had mentioned this fact.

"Yes." Rex recalled it was in Pamela Farley's statement. She had asked Sabine where she'd acquired the garment. "Anything else?" he asked Latour.

"No other remains were found around Ilet Pinel. But with ze sharks, zis is to be expected."

"The police searched the area?"

"Ah, oui, monsieur. We sent out our Sea Rescue Services at dawn. Alas, nothing."

Rex thanked Latour for the information and with sincere warmth wished him good day. But why were the gendarmes sticking to the shark theory? It could hardly do the tourist industry much good. But perhaps a shark attack, rare as they were around the island, was more acceptable than a murder. At least sharks were confined to the sea,

He decided to waste no time in going to see the influential Monsieur Bijou. Of all the people he could think of, the developer seemed to have the most clout in the investigation. Rex was all the more intrigued to meet him after what Sean O'Sullivan had said the night before, even though he doubted much of it was true. Fabulously wealthy men often had stories made up about them.

After further phone work, Rex was able to track Bijou down at his latest creation, the Marina del Mar, and arrange a meeting for that afternoon. Danielle provided him with a map and pointed to Anse Marcel where the exclusive marina resort was located. The bay, just around the coast from Ilet Pinel, as it happened, looked as though a bite had been taken out of the northernmost part of the island. It wasn't far away, and he would ask Paul Winslow to lend him his Jeep.

First, he left a message for Thaddeus in London asking him to research Monsieur Bijou's—AKA Coenraad van Bijhooven's—background, suggesting he look into possible activities in Amsterdam. Thaddeus, whose services Rex had utilized in his last case, had roomed at Oxford with an undergraduate who now worked for Interpol. If there was any dirt to dig up, Thad would likely find it, but would be doing so in his spare time. Meanwhile, Rex would meet with Bijou in person and see what could have inspired the Irishman to spin such improbable tales.

"In case I can't borrow a car, is the hotel limo available for two o'clock?" Rex asked Danielle at the desk, feeling this might be appropriate transport for his appointment.

She told him it was booked for the afternoon to take the von Muellers to Philipsburg, but she would see if the van was free. Rex said not to worry, and made his way to the Winslows' cabana. Paul unabashedly opened the door in the altogether, holding a mug of coffee.

"Sorry to bother you again, but the limo's taken and I have a meeting with Mr. Bijou. Seems a pity to monopolize the van for just one passenger..."

"No problem, dear man. Shan't be needing the Jeep today."

"In that case, I'll take it now, if I may, and do some sightseeing."

Winslow reached back to a table in the hall and pressed the car keys into Rex's hand. "Send dear Mr. Bijou our regards."

Before setting out on his trip, Rex knocked quietly at Vernon Powell's cabana, not wishing to wake him if he was still asleep. He waited a minute or two, but hearing no one stir beyond the door, hopped into Paul's Jeep and drove away from the protected and privileged grounds of La Plage d'Azur Resort.

Half an hour later, he was well on his way up the coast after stopping off for a sandwich. An unobstructed sea breeze gently blew in though the windows. What he appreciated most about St. Martin so far, he reflected, was that the island had not broken out in a rash of concrete condominium and hotel towers like so many vacation hotspots—the eastern seaboard of Florida and the Costa del Sol in Spain, to name but a few. He hoped that wouldn't change, but with developers like Bijou putting up luxury residential complexes and glitzy high-rises along the coast, who knew?

When he arrived at the Marina del Mar, he found a gated community of six towers soaring from lusciously landscaped mini-islands linked by navigable waterways with individual boat slips and Venetian-style bridges. He parked the Jeep in the underground garage of the first tower, as Bijou's personal assistant had instructed on the phone, and climbed the stairs to the first level, where he entered an air-conditioned lobby tiled in Italian marble. Classical music floated from yucca plants festooning the far corners, while a tubular aquarium in the center disappeared into the cathedral ceiling, soothing the visitor in mind and spirit with its gentle burble and lazy shoals of angelfish. Impossible to enter the calm and tasteful elegance of the Marina del Mar tower without feeling a sense of awe, Rex thought, feeling a trifle shabby by comparison in his short-sleeved white shirt and chino pants.

At a V-shaped reception desk, a young woman modeling Spock eyebrows and subtly applied mauve eye shadow supervised a chrome laptop lit up with blue keys.

"Rex Graves to see Monsieur Bijou," he informed her.

"I'll let him know you are here," she said in a neutral accent., and spoke into an intercom. "He will see you now, Mr. Graves. Please go up to the penthouse suite."

Summoning one of the transparent elevators, Rex pressed the button for the nineteenth floor. The car sped noiselessly upward and deposited him at a plush-carpeted antechamber leading to a solid-looking door. Before he had time to reach for the button, an Adonis of indeterminate race in a white dress suit and black bowtie admitted him into the suite.

"This way, sir," he murmured deferentially, leading Rex through a hall and spacious living room of ultramodern design, and onto a white balcony with panoramic vistas of the private marina and open blue sea.

A stylish man in his fifties approached, clean-shaven, and with not a silver hair out of place. His eyes were so pale as to be colorless. Even Rex, who had little interest in clothes, could tell that the custom-made suit came from the most expensive cloth, the shirt fabric was of the finest linen, and the tie of the rarest silk—platinum gold in color. Rex felt even more unhappily frumpy in the man's presence than before. As they shook hands, he detected an expensively subtle aftershave wafting from Bijou's person.

"Would you care to join me in a gin and tonic?" he asked in exquisite English that was yet not quite English.

"Thank you." Clearly, a beer was out of the question.

"Oscar, please bring the drinks upstairs."

Upstairs? Rex looked about him, certain there

couldn't be another story to the building, but Monsieur Bijou gestured to a flight of steps off the balcony, which brought them to a rooftop terrace and pool. He offered Rex one of four padded patio chairs beneath a square umbrella.

"The Marina del Mar is truly an achievement," Rex said, deciding a compliment was in order. "And the views are breathtaking."

"It was a long time in the making, but yes, I am pleased with the result." His host sat across from him and crossed his long legs. "We pre-sold ninety percent of the condominiums before we even broke ground. It is a relatively simple matter for non-nationals to buy real estate on the island. You could perhaps consider one for yourself."

In keeping with his name, Monsieur Bijou wore an ostentatious array of jewels on his manicured fingers: an opal, a sapphire, an emerald—but none on his ring finger. This was probably just as well, since Rex couldn't begin to imagine what a Madame Bijou would look like. The valet dispensed tumblers garnished with twists of lime on the table.

"Perhaps I'll consider a little *pied-à-terre* on Saint Martin when I retire," Rex said.

"Why wait? Property values will go up, and the sooner you buy, the more time you will have to enjoy it." Rex glanced politely about him in appreciation. "Indeed, there are so many opportunities here," his host pursued. "My newest project is a night club in Marigot, which will have a floor show styled after *Les Folies-Bergères*."

"With the Can-Can?"

"But of course. You approve?"

"I'm more familiar with the Highland Fling myself."

Monsieur Bijou smiled urbanely. "There is no comparison, I'm sure. Imagine beautiful, scantily clad girls in bright costumes dancing above the footlights, kicking up their legs to the sound of a live Parisian band." He waved a glittering hand as if to conjure up the vision.

"I can see it now," Rex said. The Tanqueray gin helped, adding a nice dry kick to the Schweppes.

"And so to other business. Paul Winslow said you were looking into the matter of the missing actress. How can I help?"

"It seems you've been of tremendous assistance already."

"A favour for a friend. The least I could do."

A self-interested favour, Rex surmised. Paul Winslow had rich friends who sometimes ended up purchasing property on St. Martin, and he could send them Bijou's way. "Did you hear that the rest of Sabine Durand's pareo was recovered at sea?"

"I did."

"We must pursue the investigation—"

Monsieur Bijou abruptly deposited his glass on the wrought-iron table. "What does the pareo prove?"

"That she ended up in the water. My concern is how she got there."

"Without more evidence, where do we go? The most obvious possibility is that Mademoiselle Durand slipped on the rocks and cut herself, and then foolishly went bathing in the sea at dusk when sharks come inshore to feed. No doubt you are aware how attracted these predators are to blood in the water." Bijou displayed his rings in another flourish of the hand. "My dear sir, please be at liberty to continue your inquiries, but further insistence on my part with the police would prove fruitless."

"The Gendarmerie report states she 'in all probability' drowned. It's not in the least satisfactory."

Bijou shrugged. "There have been other drownings in the area, notably at Galion Beach. Visitors go in the water to cool off and, in some cases, have been overwhelmed by the tide or else dragged out to sea by the current."

"Sabine was a good swimmer and a certified scuba diver. I really would like to ascertain the cause of death. For her family and friends."

"Without a body, we may never know for sure." Bijou drummed his chair's armrest with his resplendent fingers. Clearly, he wanted the case dropped. He'd been seen to do the right thing by his wealthy friends, and now he wished for the investigation to go away.

"Bodies dead by suspicious means are bad for business?" Rex hazarded.

"Truly, Mr. Graves, why should this be a suspicious death?" The man glanced pointedly at his Rolex.

"Just one more thing, Mr. Bijou. Did you know Sabine Durand?"

"I met her only once, last year at a party in Marigot, but she made an indelible impression. Such beauty, such poise!"

Rex knocked back the rest of his gin and tonic. "I know your time is precious." Just like everything else owned by Bijou. "Let me not take up any more of it."

His host showed him back into the condo where Oscar escorted him to the front door.

"How long have you worked for Monsieur Bijou?" Rex asked before he walked through it.

Oscar's quick, dark eyes opened wide in a challenge. No point in trying to bribe him for information, Rex realized. The young man had obviously been hired for his strength and his silence. Nothing Rex could pay him would likely compensate the valet-bodyguard for what he stood to gain—or lose—in Bijou's employment.

"Well, good day to you," he said, giving up on more answers.

"And you, sir."

Rex flew down the elevator and made his way through the sepulchral splendor of the lobby, relieved to find himself back in the Jeep. So much monetary display made him uncomfortable. He couldn't wait to get back to his own resort for a swim in the ocean and wash it all off.

"What did you think of the Marina del Mar?" Paul inquired when Rex dropped off the car keys half an hour later at the Winslows' cabana.

"Impressive."

"I'll say. A bit out of my price league, unfortunately, what with all the renovations we're having done at Swanmere Manor. And what did you make of our Monsieur Bijou?"

"Glittery. And as transparent as the diamonds on his cuff links. I got nothing out of him of any value, though. What's your take on him?"

Winslow's bland features locked in concentration as he stood naked in the doorway. "Hard to say. I've only ever met him in a formally social context. He's always been very courteous."

"Less so with me. He almost had his flunky throw me off the premises." Which would have been a breathtaking nineteen stories down.

"Crime makes for bad publicity. I suppose he's trying to protect his business interests," Winslow said.

Maybe that was not all he was trying to protect. Rex had the sneaking suspicion the police were indeed in Bijou's pocket and that he was only paying lip service to the guests at La Plage d'Azur Resort. Having now met the property developer, Rex found himself hoping that Sean O'Sullivan's gossip had substance. He would truly love to knock Midas off his ivory tower.

EIGHT

Rex wandered back to the resort's office to see if any calls had come in during his trip to Anse Marcel, but there were none. He was especially eager for background information on Bijou from Thaddeus in London. He decided to call Campbell while he was there, clearing the long-distance call with Danielle at reception and being given the code that would bill it to the cabana where he was staying.

"How's it going?" his son asked in American fashion.

Rex winced. But at least he hadn't asked, "What up?" One year in the States, and Campbell was already losing his Scottish diction.

"Good," Rex responded in like manner, eschewing the adverb grammatically required by the question.

"Have you caught the bad guy yet?"

"This is only my third day!"

"Didn't you solve that case at Swanmere, wherever it was, in three days? You must be slipping, Dad."

"Thanks for the vote of confidence. This investigation is trickier as there's no body and very few clues to go on. Actually, I wanted to ask you, since you're studying marine science: Are shark attacks common in the Caribbean?"

"Not as common as in North America or South Africa, where a combination of cold and warm waters brings a large variety of sharks," Campbell said. "The Bahamas has recorded more attacks than any other Caribbean destination, but still less than Florida."

"I hope you're being careful." Rex didn't like to think of his son surfing in Florida, yet that had been part of the attraction for Campbell in attending university there.

"It's no more dangerous than mountaineering in the Cairngorms or some other risk-taking adventures I could mention—like going after murderers."

"You have a logical argument for everything. You really should've gone into law."

"Dad, don't start on that again."

"Okay, what else can you tell me about sharks?"

"The more surf, the greater the risk of a shark mistaking a human for a fish, especially if the swimmer is wearing shiny jewelry. No, I don't wear jewelry, before you ask."

"Thank goodness for small mercies. Now, Jacques Cousteau, what can you tell me about tides?"

"Look, dad, I've got a date in a few minutes."

"Just remember who's paying for your education. Please tell me I'm not wasting my money." Rex heard his son give a put-upon sigh before launching into his explanation.

"There are usually two high tides and two low tides every day, right? With a little over six hours between high and low tide. Okay so far? The entire tidal cycle repeats itself approximately fifty minutes later each day."

Campbell relayed this information in a bored and superior tone. Rex privately forgave him because the lad was still a teenager and therefore programmed to be obnoxious.

"When the tide has reached its highest and lowest points," his son continued, "there's a brief period when there's no current ebbing or flowing, referred to as slack water. Dad, if you ever went out on boats, you'd know all this. Or you could just Google it."

"I'm no sailor—you know that. I get seasick. And I don't have ready access to smartphones and such here."

"I thought you were on Saint Martin, not a desert island."

How to explain his dad was in a nudist colony? "It's a sort of back-to-basics retreat," Rex fudged. "Glad you're learning something, son."

"Any chance you can send me some money?"

"I gave you some in Miami."

"I know, but Consuela is high and constant maintenance."

"Find a lass who's lower maintenance."

"You saw her, Dad. She's hot."

"Get a job then."

"Yeah, thanks."

Campbell was losing his Scots accent and all respect. He would never talk to his grandmother like this and risk getting walloped with her Bible. Just a year ago, he had been addressing his father as "sir," a habit ingrained by his privileged education at Fettes College in Edinburgh. Ah, well, the times they were a-changing, and perhaps just as well, Rex conceded, determined not to be a stick-in-the-mud.

"Take care, son," he said, ending the call with a smile in his voice.

Standing at the desk in the office behind reception, he whipped out the pad and pencil from his shirt pocket and wrote down some figures. The shore had been submerged at seven o'clock the previous evening when he reached the rocky promontory. Working backwards, he calculated that the tide would have been out when Sabine disappeared, leaving only wet sand. Yet there had been no mention of this in the police report.

He flipped back through his notes on the guests, beside whose names he had made annotations—further questions he needed to ask, or more information to be gathered on them from other sources. The data on Vernon Powell was spare. Sabine's husband was the one guest Rex hadn't spoken to one-on-one. The general consensus among the guests he had interviewed was that Vernon was jealous and controlling, and prone to fits of violence. Moreover, Rex had promised Winslow he would attempt to pry him out of his shell.

Making this his next priority, he walked up to the second beachfront cabana of the row but, like this morning, he got no answer to his knock at the front door. He banged louder.

"Vernon, it's Rex! I've brought your letters."

Eventually, he heard the sound of bare feet approaching on the tile hallway, and the door opened a foot wide. Vernon stuck his head out. He was shaved and clear-eyed, but gave off the unmistakable scent of rum. Strains of "If I Were a Rich Man" from *Fiddler on the Roof* tumbled through the doorway.

Musicals and opera were not Rex's cup of tea, He found both to be overly dramatic, not to mention unrealistic, in that people were not in the habit of bursting into spontaneous song in everyday life. If he did that in court, he would be summarily disbarred and committed to a mental asylum.

"Thanks," Vernon said, taking the day's mail.

"I thought we could have dinner tonight."

Sabine's husband paused for a second, and Rex thought he would find an excuse to refuse. "As long as it's not at The Cockatoo," he said drily.

"Wherever you recommend."

"The California in Grand Case. Good food, great view, and big enough to where we're not likely to run into any of this crowd."

"Right you are. I'll arrange for the resort to limo us over at seven, if that suits."

That gave Rex enough time for a bit of relaxation. He'd been looking forward to a swim all afternoon, and felt he had earned it. Returning to his own cabana, he changed into his Bermudas and applied a liberal amount of sunscreen. The beach attendants were collapsing the giant yellow umbrellas for the day by the time he arrived, although many sunbathers lingered in the soft sunshine, chatting on towels and loungers over cocktails, reading books and magazines, or simply gazing out over the gently undulating expanse of azure sea beneath a deep blue sky.

Rex met the Irvings jogging back from the village side of the beach along the firmer sand along the waterline. Neither had so much as broken into a sweat. They slowed down to a stop.

"Hey, Rex. Haven't seen you all day." Dick, only slightly out of breath, had not a stitch on except for a red and white bandanna. A Yin-Yang symbol, which put Rex in mind of two embracing tadpoles, was tattooed on his smooth chest.

"I've been busy. I went to Anse Marcel to meet with Monsieur Bijou."

"Does he flaunt as many jewels as they say?" Penny asked, cool as a cucumber but for a slight sheen on her nose and between her tanned breasts.

"Aye, practically every gemstone you can imagine." With a shiver of distaste, Rex recalled the man's unusually pale eyes and cool, dry handshake.

"He's quite a legend. I heard he's immaculately groomed and has his own masseur. Sabine said he was bi."

"Did Sabine know him well?" Rex asked in surprise. Bijou had distinctly said he'd only met her the one time.

"Perhaps not *that* well," Penny said.

"Incidentally, I wanted to ask you both what time you got back from your trip to Saint Barts a week ago

Tuesday."

Dick questioned his wife with a glance. "I wrote down the time in my statement. Let's see—must've been around six-thirty."

"Closer to seven," Penny corrected him. "We had to wait for a cab, remember?"

"You don't have your own transport?" Rex asked.

"No, we mainly hang out here and take advantage of the beach."

"Did you take a cab to Oyster Pond that morning?"

"Yeah," Dick said. "What we tip Pascal is almost as much as a cab fare."

"And you didn't get back in time for Paul's birthday dinner?"

"We might've managed it but we were pooped. In any case, we'd already told the others not to expect us before coffee, knowing it would be tight since we had to shower and change first, and there might be transport delays. At around ten, Dave and Toni knocked at our door to see if Sabine was with us, but we hadn't seen her all day."

"We went out and looked for her," Penny added.

"Were you worried?"

Penny pulled the band from her ponytail and redid it. "Not really. I thought she'd forgotten about Paul's dinner and just gone off somewhere. I remember being annoyed. She was the sort of person who always has to be center stage and create drama around her."

"Yeah, I felt bad for Paul," Dick elaborated. "At least we told him we might not be coming. None of the guests were exactly sober, so the search effort probably wasn't very efficient. They just wandered about calling her name. Penny and me kinda took over and got the guards from the resort to check out the beach on the other side of the rocks."

"I'll need to speak with them."

"They're nice local boys," Penny said. "Not too cop-like. They mainly just keep out the riff-raff."

As she spoke, a guard in khaki uniform paced along the sand, a club secured in his belt.

"You get the odd voyeur and dope peddler on the beach," Dick explained, watching the guard. "Security only patrols the beach once the umbrella attendants have left. During the day, one guard stays up by the cabanas."

Rex thanked the Irvings for the information and waded into the shallows. Fewer people remained now on the beach, and still less in the sea. Most would be headed back to their hotels to prepare for dinner or a night on the town. None of the other guests from his resort were in evidence. Standing waist deep in the warm water, he gazed at the tiny fish swirling about the sandy bottom. Then, launching himself headlong, he free-styled to the raft anchored in the bay and hoisted himself up the ladder.

The waning sun bathed his face as, from the wooden platform, he surveyed the eight cabanas peeping through the coconut palms and clumps of sea grape, which divided them from the beach. Someone at the resort must know more about Sabine Durand than they were willing to tell. It was simply a matter of probing, applying pressure along the airtight seam until the case cracked open like a walnut, exposing the dusky secret within. It appeared Sabine's husband might be ready to crack.

NINE

The waterfront restaurant resembled a warehouse in size and structure, which lent a nice airy feel. The entrance displayed shelves of island souvenirs and offered a grouping of sofas where couples sat with drinks from the bar.

"My usual table," Vernon Powell requested of the maître d', who led them to one of the large twilit windows open to the shushing sound of waves on the beach. The lights of the British island of Anguilla twinkled in the distance.

Rex complimented Vernon on his choice of restaurant. Scanning the menu, he decided on the hot artichoke in goat cheese sauce au gratin followed by coquilles St. Jacques on curried pasta. After consulting with Vernon, he ordered a bottle of Sancerre. "As you were saying in the limo about the resort manager…," he prompted when the waiter left.

"Greg Hastings was at Paul's birthday party at The Cockatoo all evening. He organized champagne and cake on the house, and sat down with us for dinner."

"Unlikely he could have slipped away then."

"No," Vernon said. "Anyway, I don't suspect him for a minute. He's managed the resort ever since most of us have been going to the Plage—fifteen years in my case, even after my first wife died. It was less lonely than going on a singles' cruise or to Club Med."

"And the driver?"

"Pascal is just as professional, and has worked there for quite a few years as well."

While chauffeuring them over to Grand Case, Pascal had told Rex that before his job at the resort, he'd worked for a charter boat company, sailing many types of luxury craft for weeks on end all over the Caribbean. Now he got to sleep most nights at home. He lived in town with his wife and four children, and having the evening off the Tuesday Sabine disappeared, had been fishing on his boat until past sunset with his two eldest.

"You should be looking at Brook," Vernon said, wielding his crab cracker, which he then clamped on the crustacean's claw. With one snap, the delicate pink meat was laid bare. "There's an edge to Brook that's not immediately obvious. He has incredible drive. Fact is, he couldn't have made it to where he is today without being ruthless when he needed to be."

I'm sure the same could be said of you, Rex reflected.

"He was crazy about Sabine." Vernon wiped his fingers off on his napkin. "Well, everybody was."

The women not so much, Rex thought.

"D'you think you'll ever get to the bottom of this case?"

"I certainly intend to try," Rex said, piqued by his dinner companion's tone. "I'm still at the fact-finding stage. It might help if I could take a look at your wife's personal belongings. Not that I wish to impose on your grief..."

"Feel free. I've left everything the way it was. I guess at the back of my mind I keep thinking she'll come back."

"Did she ever take anything with her on her walk?"

"Just what she was wearing, I imagine. How are your scallops?"

Rex was not so easily thrown off the scent. "How was the marriage? Sorry to have to ask."

Vernon took a deep breath. "Look, I want to find out what happened to my wife, however painful it might be, but with regard to your question, I didn't feel married to Sabine. She did more or less what she pleased."

"Extramarital affairs?"

"She said not."

"Did the question of divorce ever come up?"

"It did. Sabine traveled a lot for her work and I took frequent trips to LA. Distance can put a strain on a marriage."

"I expect, as an attorney, you put a prenuptial agreement in place?"

Something resembling a smile cracked Vernon's wooden face. "Of course. She wasn't very far along in her career when I met her."

"And, under the terms of the divorce agreement, how would Sabine have fared?"

"Badly."

Rex was left in no doubt that being on the wrong side of Vernon Powell would be an extremely uncomfortable place to be. "Where was home when you were together?"

"At our apartment on Park Avenue. Our month here was supposed to give us a chance to rekindle the romance."

During the rest of the main course, they concentrated on the meal.

The young waiter cleared away their dinner plates. "Would you care for dessert?" he inquired, and listed the selection.

"Why does food always sound so much better in French?" Rex asked in appreciation. Although on a self-imposed diet, he decided to make an exception since the food was so good. "I'll take the Crêpes Suzette."

Vernon ordered profiteroles, and the waiter glided away.

"I don't get to eat like this very often back home," Rex said.

"What is the national dish in Scotland?"

"We're rather fond of our haggis and pulverized turnip."

"Haggis?"

"Sheep's innards."

"Good Lord." Vernon pulled a sour face.

"The Scots are a thrifty lot. None of the sheep goes to waste."

Their waiter drew up a tripod table equipped with

a hibachi and set fire to the pancakes in the brass skillet. A decadent fragrance of torched orange brandy and caramelized sugar wafted into the air. Rex wished he could bottle it and spray it onto his pillow.

Vernon sliced into his chocolate-topped pastry filled with French custard. "You can spend a month here and eat out at a different gourmet restaurant every day without ever going into Marigot of Philipsburg."

"Add to that the fantastic weather and Caribbean Sea. It's paradise all right." Or was, until Sabine Durand went missing, which did lend a sinister pall to the attractions. "Did Sabine take medication of any kind?"

"Only Luminal to help combat jet lag and stage fright."

"What was she seeing the chiropractor about?"

"She got thrown by a horse when she was fourteen and was laid up for a while. Her back still played up from time to time. She said the quack in Philipsburg worked wonders."

"Did you ever go with her?"

Vernon shook his head. "It would've meant a wait at his office and then a shopping expedition afterward. She was always gone at least three hours."

"Did she suffer from depression?"

"She didn't kill herself, if that's what you're getting at."

Rex did not press the point. "How did you come to lose your phone on the beach that night?"

"I didn't. It was in our cabana. I remember checking my messages before I went on the dive excursion.

Later, I couldn't find it anywhere."

"This was before the party?"

"Yes, while waiting for my wife to make an appearance," Vernon said tersely. "In the end, I left without her."

The sommelier poured them the rest of the white wine from the ice bucket. Vernon thawed slightly when they moved away from the topic of Sabine to discuss the differences between American and Scottish law, interested to learn that courts in Scotland have fifteen jurors.

"Another important distinction," Rex told him, "is that in our law every essential fact has to be corroborated by at least two independent witnesses."

"Harder to prove guilt," the New York entertainment attorney said.

"Aye, but our law allows three verdicts: guilty, not guilty, and not-proven. Not-proven means that though the prosecution failed to meet the criterion of 'beyond reasonable doubt,' there's still a suspicion of guilt in the jury's mind and in the mind of the public."

"That's how I feel—as though my friends were the jury and I'm walking around in a cloud of suspicion."

"We'll see if we can't clear that up," Rex said. *You canny old lawyer.*

The limousine picked them up at nine prompt.

"I'll be playing racquet ball with Duke in the morning at eight," Vernon informed Rex on the drive back to the resort. "You can come to my cabana then and poke around to your heart's content."

"Thanks. It'll give me a better feel for Sabine."

"I wish you could've met her."

"I do too. She sounds intriguing."

They bid each other a cordial goodnight. When Rex opened his door, Brooklyn met him in the hallway and handed him a message from the front desk.

"I found this on the front door," his roommate said. "It says it's urgent. I was about to go looking for you."

"I went to dinner in Grand Case." Thinking the message might be from Thaddeus in London, Rex was eager to read it. Inside it said, *"Call mother."*

"Want to use my cell phone?"Brooklyn asked.

Rex glanced at his watch, rubbing it absent-mindedly with his thumb. "It's past two in the morning in Scotland."

"But if it's urgent..."

"Aye, thanks. I'm not getting good service on mine out here."

"You'll have to take it outside to get a decent signal," Brooklyn said, handing him the Motorola. "Just don't let anyone see you. They're a bit uptight around here about nude pictures of themselves showing up on some sleazy website and being blackmailed. Hope everything's okay," he added before disappearing into his bedroom.

The message had been taken almost three hours ago, past his mother's bedtime. Anxiously, he dialed her number.

"This is the Graves residence...," the housekeeper in Edinburgh intoned on the recording.

Rex started speaking in the hope his mother would

pick up. If the news was that urgent, she would have waited up for his call—although at eighty-five years old, she was prone to nodding off after dinner. "I'll try you first thing in the morning my time, Mother," he ended by saying into the machine.

He wandered back in from the patio and knocked at Brooklyn's door to return the phone.

"Couldn't get through?" the American asked, tying the belt of his white bathrobe.

"I got the answering machine."

"Keep the phone with you so you can try again later. Leave it on the kitchen counter when you're done."

"I appreciate it. My mother will be up in three or four hours. The message might be regarding my lady friend in Iraq. She went on a humanitarian mission out there, and I haven't been able to reach her in weeks, either where she's staying or at the relief office."

"That's tough," Brooklyn said sympathetically. "Here, let me make you a pot of coffee. Looks like it's going to be a long night."

Rex followed him into the tiled living room, simply but stylishly furnished in rattan and beige-and-yellow padded sofas and armchairs. "You really don't need to go to the trouble."

"No trouble." Brooklyn filled the machine and within minutes the kitchen was filled with an appetizing aroma of freshly ground French roast. He leaned against the counter. "Have you contacted your Embassy?"

"Aye. Moira's not on any casualty list and hasn't been reported missing."

Brooklyn pulled two mugs from an upper cabinet. "I heard you had a son in Florida..."

"Campbell. He just finished his first year at university in Jacksonville. Marine Science."

"Cool. Milk, sugar?"

"Both—thanks."

Brooklyn set a mug of steaming coffee on the counter beside Rex and poured one for himself. "My one regret is not having kids," he said. "Once I meet the right woman, I will though."

"Did no one ever fit that description?" Rex didn't want to seem to be prying into Brooklyn's love life, but the companionship fostered by the urgent message from his mother, the time of night, and the two of them sharing a cabana in the French West Indies made him forego his usual reserve.

"If you mean Sabine," Brooklyn said candidly, "there was never any question of kids for her. She said she wasn't built for it. Well, you saw in the photo how skinny she was."

"Many a brawny bairn was born of a slender lass," Rex countered. "When Fiona, my late wife, was carrying Campbell, the doctor warned she might have to have a C-section due to her having narrow hips. But she was swiftly delivered of an eight-pound boy without the necessity for surgical intervention."

She had failed to win the battle against breast cancer, however. Rex gulped his coffee to force down the bitter lump rising in his throat.

"In any case," Brooklyn said, "kids would have gotten in the way of Sabine's career."

"Moira has often talked about adopting a child. She said not to be surprised if she brought one back from Iraq."

"How would you feel about that?"

"Just fine." Rex swirled the coffee dregs at the bottom of his mug. What he said was true enough, but he wondered if even raising an orphan would ultimately fulfill Moira's indefatigable capacity for self-sacrifice. There had been times when he felt unable to keep up.

"Vernon would have liked to have kids, I think," Brooklyn said, pouring the remains of his coffee down the sink. "Have you had a chance to speak with him yet?"

"We spoke over dinner. He's an astute man."

"Yeah, not so easy to manipulate. Sabine couldn't exactly twist him around her little finger the way she could other men."

Yawning uncontrollably, Rex took another look at his watch. "I'll try to grab a couple of hours' sleep and then call my mother again. Thanks for the loan of your phone."

"Hey, don't sweat it. Wake me up if you need to talk."

Rex thanked him and went to prepare for bed. It was a horrible feeling to crave sleep, yet know you might be unable to succumb to its blissful release. He switched on the ceiling fan, lay down on his bed, and turned off the light. He lay there tensely, his mind dancing to any tune his thoughts struck up, morbid ones where a blindfolded Moira was being held at gunpoint by terrorists or, on another ominous note, his mother had been diagnosed with a terminal illness. Or perhaps Miss Bird, their devoted housekeeper, had taken a fall down the stairs.

Rex rolled over on his side. He could just make out the outline of Helen's postcard on the nightstand. A soothing melody calmed his nerves as he recalled her words:*...went ahead and booked my passage on the Sun-Fun Cruise Line. Will dock at St. Martin on the 23rd of July. Meet me off the Olympia...*

He fell asleep at that point, but tossed fretfully for the next couple of hours, the import of the late-night call from his mother threading darkly through his troubled dreams.

TEN

At five-thirty Rex awoke with a start. Jumping off the bed, he stumbled onto the back patio and dialed his mother's number in Edinburgh. It was so quiet outside he could hear the lapping of waves on the white sugar sand beyond the grayed-down colors of the predawn.

"Mother," he almost shouted at the sound of her voice. "I tried calling last night."

"How are ye, Reginald? You sound croaky. Are ye coming down wi' something?"

"I just got up. I've been worried sick—"

"It isna bad, I dinna think."

"What isn't?" Rex asked, experiencing a meteoric rise in his blood pressure.

"A letter arrived from Iraq."

"What does it say?"

"Well, I didna open it! It's addressed to you."

"Oh, fer goodness' sake, open it, will ye?" Rex said, emotion thickening his Scots accent. His hand on the cell phone started shaking. He gripped it more tightly.

"Are ye sure?"

"Mother," he said in a stern voice. He heard the tearing of paper at the other end of the connection and then a lengthy pause. "Is it a long letter?" he asked. And why a letter?

"Noo, it's just that Moira writes that..."

"What?" His mother's reticence alarmed him. Perhaps Moira had uncharacteristically added some intimate language to her missive, and his mother was standing in the hall, stricken with shock. Sex was never a topic of conversation in the house.

"She's run off!" his mother said in disbelief.

"Run off where?" Moira was already in Iraq. How much farther could she run?

"Run off wi' another man!"

"Who?"

"A photographer for an American paper."

"Mother, read me the letter."

"Well, I shall, but it's shameful. She writes, 'Dearest Rex, please forgive me for not writing before. I tried so many times, but it was not easy to say what I had to, and the pressure of work here is enormous, as you know. More on that later. I've met someone. We didn't mean for it to happen, but it did and—'"

"That's enough. I get the picture."

"Aye, well. There's no even a return address. So, what's it like oot there on Saint Martin?" his mother asked in an obvious attempt to distract him.

Rex got hold of himself. "There are bays with powdery sand beaches and palm trees," he replied without enthusiasm, averting his eyes from the blaze of yellow just now breaking through the amber sky. "It's straight out of *Treasure Island*. The food is mostly spicy or French, sometimes a mixture of both."

"It sounds so exotic."

"It is," Rex said with a despondent sigh.

"I am sorry aboot Moira."

"Aye, but it's still better than finding out she was hurt." Just barely.

"What aboot that nice woman who called from Derby? The one you met at Christmas. She sounded so pleasant on the phone."

"Helen d'Arcy. She's stopping off on Saint Martin for a day. She's on a Caribbean cruise."

"Well then. I have to say I'm verra disappointed in Moira Wilcox. Running off wi' a photographer! The ones on TV all look so scruffy. And she's so straight-laced. I just canna credit it. But I'm glad you're taking it so well. When are ye going to bring Helen to tea?"

"I'll have to see how things go when I see her."

"It may all turn oot for the best," his mother said cheerfully. "Have ye been in touch wi' Campbell."

"We spoke yesterday. He sends his love."

"I wish the lad would write more."

"He probably would if he could e-mail you."

"E-mail! At my age."

She was incapable even of working the television remote. Imagining her in front of a laptop was as incongruous as picturing a robot taking tea at a table set with his mother's lace doilies.

"Reginald?"

"Mother?"

"Reread the Gospel according to Matthew, chapter eleven, verses twenty-eight through thirty. It will make your suffering easier to bear."

"Aye, Mother."

In the event, he did not resort to the scriptures. Leaving Brooklyn's phone on the kitchen counter, he strode back through the sliding glass doors in a frigid blue fury. The sand felt cool beneath his pounding feet. He barely noticed when he stood on a burr. The beach, deserted and devoid of the vibrant color of later morning, looked less welcoming, but the water was just beginning to glimmer with promise. He ripped off his pajamas, abandoning them on the shore, and splashed into the sea as fast as the resistance of the water permitted.

We didn't mean for it to happen, but it did.

Moira's echoing words infuriated him. What sort of excuse was that? He'd managed to resist Helen's amorous advances at Christmas. He swam parallel to the beach, his strokes tugging the sea out of the way as he furiously blinked salt from his eyes. When he reached the promontory, he U-turned under the water and made his way back the way he had come, using the cabanas as a landmark, the vigorous exercise gradually driving all meaningful thought from his brain.

Feeling better, he flung his upright legs through the shallows to where his cotton pj's lay unceremoniously tossed on the sand. Realizing he had forgotten his towel, he used them to dry off his body. He spotted Paul and Elizabeth on their patio at the third cabana and gave a quick wave back before hurrying on to his own bungalow, clutching his striped bottoms in front of him. He'd forgotten the Winslows were early risers.

After rinsing off under the outdoor shower, he went inside to shave, and then lingered over a Sudoku puzzle while drinking his coffee. Solving it took longer than usual since his mind kept wandering back to Moira. He still had trouble believing the news.

Brooklyn wandered onto the patio in his bathrobe, yawning and stretching. He looked even better with dark stubble—like a Hollywood pirate—Rex noticed with envy. His own chin sprouted graying ginger hairs and he had bedhead first thing in the morning.

"There's fresh coffee in the pot," he informed Brooklyn.

"Thanks. Did you get your news?"

"Aye, nobody died but me. My girlfriend left me for another man—a photographer. One of you lot." Rex explained about the Dear John letter, and tried to make light of the matter.

"Plenty more fish in the sea," Brooklyn commiserated.

When eight o'clock rolled around, Rex went next door and, poking his head into Vernon's hallway, called out "Hello!" to see of the lawyer had left for his game of racquet ball.

Hearing no response, he entered the cabana and glanced around the living room, furnished much the same as Brooklyn's, but with beige-and-burgundy soft furnishings. He opened the door to one of the two bedrooms, to all appearances uninhabited and with the bed neatly made, but when he looked in the wall-to-wall closet, he found a rack of women's apparel. He doubted these could belong to Sabine. Though stylish enough, most of the dresses didn't live up to what he pictured a glamorous young actress would wear. There were no high-end designer labels like Prada or Emanuel or von Furstenberg, big names that even he would recognize. The size of one evening dress caught his eye, surely too large for such a willowy lass. Perhaps she had put on weight since the riding photo Brooklyn had shown him.

Or perhaps she was expecting to. What if the chiropractor she was seeing in Philipsburg was another sort of doctor? Whatever was going on, Vernon seemed unaware of it. Rex decided to leave the questions for now and continue his search.

The built-in safe in the master closet was, of course, locked. Rex examined the jewelry on the dressing table. Nothing of great value here. No personal effects of sentimental value either, anywhere, belonging to Sabine.

Next he searched the bathroom, again finding nothing of note, only the usual male and female toiletries. Little the wiser than before he arrived, Rex headed toward the front entrance. As he was leaving, a statuesque woman in her forties with handsome ebony features, approached, rolling a cleaning cart along the path. On it were stacked folded towels and a supply of the lemon sherbet bar soap provided courtesy of the resort.

"Okay to go in?" she asked.

Rex held the door open for her. "Aye, no one's

home."

Afraid she might think he'd been snooping, which in effect he had, he was about to explain his presence.

"Is maid service to Monsieur's satisfaction?" she asked.

"Oh, aye. The cabanas are spotless."

Outside, he caught sight of a guard patrolling the far perimeter of the resort. Rex crossed the grounds.

A six-foot chain-link fence concealed by a flowering hedge closed off the property from the open land beyond, which ended at the dirt road leading to the Sundown Ranch and Butterfly Farm.

"Mind if I walk with you?" he asked the beefy guard.

"I seen you around. You dat lawyer from Scotland." He introduced himself as Winston and said he'd be glad to answer any questions.

Rex fell into step with him as he toured the outdoor tennis and indoor racquet ball courts. "How many guards work here?"

Winston informed him there were six, who rotated. He then volunteered the information that he and a man called Pierre had been working the night shift when Sabine Durand disappeared. He said they'd arrived for work shortly before six and went to the front office as usual, where the desk manager gave them a briefing before they went on patrol. The Gendarmerie sent reports to the resort about any crime in the area, and the guards were told what to look out for.

"Was it quiet that night?" Rex asked.

"Very quiet. I din' know what was up till da Canadian man with tattoos come running up an' say we have to search for da young lady. Pierre an' me went past da rocks out dere." Winston pointed in the general direction. "Was too dark to see much, but dere wasn't no body. Next morning I had to stay till da po-lice come."

It transpired that Winston had been the one to find Vernon's cell phone. When asked about Pierre's activities that night, he told Rex that on patrol they walk a circle, one on resort grounds, the other beachside, and they meet up in the middle and continue. Every five rounds, they stop for a cigarette break at The Cockatoo by the kitchens. After ten o'clock they're given a meal there. He was headed over that Tuesday night when Dick Irving alerted him about the missing woman.

When Rex spoke to Pierre, on guard at the main entrance to the resort, the shy youth repeated everything Winston had said. He hadn't understood whom they were looking for until he saw the papers the next day and recognized Mlle. Durand.

"Any strange goings-on here in the last couple of weeks that you remember?"

Pierre shook his head, a blank look on his face. Rex thanked him and went inside the main building where he was pleased to find a message from Thaddeus waiting for him at the front desk, saying to call him in London. At last!

ELEVEN

"Browne, Quiggley, and Squire," the young law clerk answered. "Mr. Quiggley's office."

"Thad, 'tis I," Rex announced.

"Oh, good, sir. I have the information you required. Here are the salient facts. I'll forward the entire report once we're off the phone."

Rex heard a preparatory cough. Thaddeus was still a bit wet behind the ears, but he was a thorough researcher.

"Coenraad van Bijhooven, alias Bijou," the law clerk began, "was born in Amsterdam in nineteen fifty-seven. His mother, Alice Frankel, was a high-class call girl who married Henrick van Bijhooven, a successful industrialist, whom she abandoned along with their son when Coenraad was five. She emigrated to America with another man. Coenraad went on to read law at the Sorbonne."

"Did he now?" Rex asked pensively, pacing in front of the office desk, phone pressed to his ear. "Go on."

"Upon his return to Holland, he opened a string of

clubs in the Amsterdam red light district. His father died, leaving him a pile of money which provided capital for Coenraad's more ambitious projects on Saint Martin."

"Were you able to link him to the Jewel Murders in Amsterdam?"

"A couple of witnesses came forward at the time pointing the finger at him, but they must have been intimidated or bought off, because ultimately they never appeared in court. The victims had all worked for Coenraad as exotic dancers—and such." Thaddeus gave a discreet cough. "All were of slender build with long red or brown hair and delicately modeled cheekbones."

Rex froze. The description immediately evoked an image of Sabine.

"The women resembled his mother," Thaddeus informed him. "There's a picture in the file."

"Is she still alive?"

"She passed away in the States at around the time Coenraad was studying in Paris. I don't think he ever saw her again after she left Holland when he was a child."

"Have there been any murders on the island similar to those in Amsterdam?"

"Two years ago. Two women apparently strangled but not otherwise assaulted. Both investigations fizzled out. It was widely reported a tourist was responsible who then left the island. The victims weren't found immediately. Their relative states of decomposition showed they were murdered within a couple of weeks of each other."

"Who were they?"

"One worked at The Stiletto, a gentleman's club in Philipsburg."

A chill ran down Rex's spine, alerting him to the fact he might be on to something. "Owned by Bijou?"

"Correct. He changed his name legally before he left the Netherlands, and now travels on his new passport."

"What do we know about these two girls?"

"Leona Couch was in her twenties, British. The other was a local tour guide: Geraldine Linder, early thirties. Both fit descriptions of the women in Amsterdam."

"Any connection between Geraldine Linder and Bijou?"

"None was ever established. And I don't know if semi-precious stones were found on these two women. How do you want me to send the report, sir?"

"There's a fax machine here. I didn't bring my laptop with me."

"I'll mark it for your attention with 'CONFIDENTIAL' stamped all over it. Stand by."

Rex thought Thaddeus should have gone into the Secret Service—the studious young man was clearly enjoying this project. He gave him the office fax number.

"I'll wait by the machine. And thank you so much, Thad. Next time I'm in London, I'll take Quig out to dinner and extol your virtues."

Thomas Quiggley, a partner at the firm Thaddeus

clerked for, was an old friend of Rex's.

"I'd appreciate that, Mr. Graves, sir. And good luck with the case. I hope you'll let me know the outcome."

"Never fear. Take care, lad."

For a brief moment, Rex whimsically thought how nice it would have been to have had a second son, one like Thaddeus, whom he could have mentored in law.

He exited the office and addressed Danielle at the desk. "Would you be kind enough to make an appointment for me with this chiropractor while I wait for a fax?" Handing her the message slip that had been in Vernon's pigeon-hole, he returned to the machine which was just beginning to spurt out the pages of Thad's report.

"The phone number for the chiropractor in Philipsburg does not exist," Danielle told him when he came back out of the office, report in hand.

"Are you sure it was taken down correctly?"

"*Absoluement, monsieur*. I took the number down on several occasions."

"Do you have a directory handy?"

Danielle placed the "Yellow Pages Sint Maarten" for the Dutch side of the island on the front desk. Rex scanned the listings for Dr. Sganarelle. It was an unusual surname and hard to miss, but he found no one by that name. He then checked the local phone book to no avail.

"Thanks," he said, closing it. Strange, indeed...

Entering the store located in the building, he encountered Greg Hastings, the resort manager, who wore a brass badge to that effect. A nattily dressed man with a neatly trimmed salt-and-pepper beard, he greeted Rex effusively and asked how he was enjoying his stay at La Plage d'Azur Resort.

"Most pleasant, but as I'm sure you're aware, I'm here to look into the disappearance of one of your guests." Rex asked the manager about the two guards he'd spoken with that morning.

"The employees are all carefully vetted," Hastings assured him a northern English accent. "Uh-oh," he said glancing out the window. "Rain's coming. But it doesn't usually last long."

Rex looked out at the sky, which was ominously dark to the east. Heavy raindrops began to fall and streak down the glass. "Winston told me he was the one who found the phone belonging to Mr. Powell."

"That's right. I put it in the office safe overnight. The gendarmes confiscated it the next morning but returned it a few days later after Mr. Powell insisted he needed it for work." The manager's pale face colored slightly.

Rex waited expectantly for an admission of some sort.

"I'm afraid you're going to think very badly of me."

"I'm all ears," Rex encouraged him, hoping for a promising lead.

"Well..." Hastings stuck his hands in his jacket pockets. "While I had the phone, I was curious to see what big-shot entertainment clients Mr. Powell might have. Just a quick look, mind—at his contacts list. The phone wasn't locked, curiously enough." As if that was an open invitation for him to read what was on it,

Rex thought.

The manager paused, as if waiting to be asked to divulge what he'd found, but Rex had little interest in American stars, except perhaps for Angelina Jolie.

"Anyway," Hastings continued. "A photo came up on the phone." He had the grace to cough in apology for his snooping. "Most of them were sightseeing pictures. And rock formations. Mr. Powell likes geology, it seems."

He would, Rex thought, being so stony-faced himself.

"I downloaded this particular photo because it looked suspicious to me. It was the last one taken before the phone was found on the beach, you see, and was dated July ten. Lieutenant Latour never pursued it. Perhaps he failed to see the relevance, but I have a copy on my phone." Hastings produced a slim cell phone from his breast pocket. "See what you make of this."

Rex examined the photo and enlarged it on the small screen. Taken at night, it looked at first glance like a grainy blur of indistinct shapes. "I can't make out what it is," he said holding it away from him to see if that helped.

"Look carefully."

Rex blinked to refresh his eyes and get a different perspective. "Ah, now I see," he said. "It's part of a woman's face taken from below. I recognize the Greek pattern on the necklace."

"It belongs to Mrs. Winslow. I don't think she meant to be in the photo, not from that angle."

The digital date stamp confirmed the photo was taken the day Sabine disappeared, but not at what time. What was Elizabeth's image doing on Vernon's cell phone that night of all nights? Rex asked Hastings at what time Winston found the phone.

"At ten twenty-four. If Mrs. Winslow found the phone, why did she leave it up by the rocks?"

"Good question." Pondering this new development, Rex made his purchases at the small grocery store. On his way out of the main building, he saw Duke Farley hurrying over from the direction of the racquet ball court in a jock-strap, a white towel draped around his squat neck.

"Good work-out?" Rex called out from the top step, just as the rain started in earnest, drumming on the tin porch roof.

Duke ran up the steps for cover. "You bet. Double game. D'you play?" The curly blond hair on his thick torso glistened with moisture.

"I have no eye-hand coordination."

"What do you do for exercise?"

"I like to hike and nature-watch? Birds and deer," Rex added too late.

A leering grin spread over the Texan's ruddy face. "Nature, huh? Well, you sure came to the right place.

Rex failed to understand what an intelligent woman like Pam saw in Duke Farley, but apparently the oil and beef man was worth billions.

"Yessir, plenty of bathing beauties at the Plage. Now, Sabine, there's a gal that looked good wet?"

"Excuse me?"

"The true test of beauty. Some women just look good wet."

"Oh—aye." The vision of Ursula Andress emerging seductively from the sea, blonde hair slicked back as droplets of water beaded her womanly form, had fueled many a moment of lonely adolescent lust when Rex first watched the James Bond movie.

"Shame she's no longer with us," Duke said, shaking his large head. "What'll you do if you find out who the murderer is?"

"Hand him or her over to the proper authorities."

"Give him five minutes with me first," Duke growled. "Oh, hell, this rain might last a while. See ya around." Pulling the towel over his head, he plowed into the deluge.

Rex munched on a croissant while he decided whether to make a run for it too. He didn't much like running. In any case, he lacked the energy after a short and disturbed night's sleep. He refused to dwell further on Moira. He had an important case to consider.

What was a photograph of Elizabeth Winslow doing on Vernon's phone? What if Sabine was Bijou's latest victim in a string of bizarre killings spanning from Holland to the Caribbean? Had the fabulously wealthy real estate magnate left his sparkling calling card on her as on other young women? Perhaps a gleaming aquamarine the color of Sabine's eyes, as Pam Farley had described them...

TWELVE

Rex cadged a ride into Philipsburg in Brooklyn's jeep, a newer Japanese model than Paul Winslow's, though no more roomy inside.

"Where did you say you wanted to be dropped off?" Brooklyn asked on the way to the Dutch capital.

"The Stiletto Club."

His roommate glanced over in surprise. "I don't think it's open at lunchtime. It's not one of those seedy dives either. You have to wear a suit and tie to get in."

Rex was wearing a casual short-sleeved shirt. "I'm not going for my own pleasure" He'd only ever been to one such club, and that had been for a college friend's stag night in Glasgow, a less than glamorous experience best forgotten. "I'm following a lead. Sounds like you might know where I can find the place."

"It's not far from the port."

Natural that a young bachelor of the world like Brooklyn Chalmers would know The Stiletto, Rex supposed.

They entered the narrow streets of the commercial

district and became ensnared in stop-and-go traffic. Office workers and businessmen crossed between the stalled cars. No one appeared to be in a hurry.

"What are the girls like there?" he asked Brooklyn. "I'm only asking because I heard one of them was murdered a few years ago."

"Couldn't really tell you. That's one of Bijou's joints and I tend to avoid him."

"Why's that?"

"I was seeing a young woman called Gerry from this side of the island. I even brought her to the Plage once or twice. That was two years ago. Anyway, I found out she was two-timing me with that effeminate jerk Bijou, and I thought maybe he was getting information about me from her."

"So you ended the relationship?"

"Ships passing in the night. No big deal." Brooklyn pulled into a small parking lot by a government building. "I'll have to drop you off here as I'm late for my meeting. The Stiletto is down that street all the way to your left. How will you get back to the resort?"

"I'll call the hotel desk when I'm finished, or else get a cab. See you back there."

He followed the directions Brooklyn had given him and arrived at the club, a whitewashed building wedged between two office blocks and displaying a black high-heeled shoe across the white double doors. Which turned out to be locked.

He hadn't called in advance, not wishing to alert Mr. Bijou of his intention to nose around and question some of his minions. Coming later when people would be too busy to talk to him had not made sense either, so now he was pretty much stuck as to how to proceed—until he noticed a small side door for deliveries. He turned the handle and this door opened.

Following a narrow corridor to the back of the building, he ended up in a kitchen equipped with gleaming stainless steel surfaces and cookware. A double swing door led into a restaurant decked out in elegant black-on-crimson decor, with spotlights focused on three daises for the dancers, one featuring a golden pole reaching to the ceiling. A polished cherry wood counter extended the width of the back wall. At the bar sat a man poring over a computerized ledger. Rex coughed politely to announce his presence, and the man spun around on the barstool.

"Are you lost?" he asked sternly with a faint accent, no doubt assuming Rex had wandered in off the street, and annoyed at being disturbed.

"I'm not a tourist. I came to ask a few questions regarding Mr. Bijou."

"You are from the police?"

"I'm a lawyer pursuing an investigation on behalf of a friend." Rex handed him his business card.

The man, tanned and in his mid to late thirties, looked unimpressed.

"And you are?" Rex asked.

"Erik, the bar manager."

"Erik, I need to know one thing: where your boss was on Tuesday evening, the tenth of July."

"Here."

"Are you sure?"

"Actually, yes. I have him on security video entering the building. You are quite welcome to see it." Erik glanced around him and, satisfied they were alone, said in a low voice, "Look, I don't owe him any favours other than my paycheck. And I'm not covering for the guy. Every other Tuesday evening he comes in at six, looks over the books, and stays for the show. He's due in this week, so I'm going over the accounts to make sure they're in order. Any anomalies, he'll find them. He has X-ray vision."

"I know, I met him."

"How do I know you are not really a reporter?"

"Why would I be?"

"We get them all the time. Bijou is newsworthy. He's always doing something for the community or hanging out with the elite. People like Donald Trump and—"

"Aye, Mr. Bijou seems to keep quite busy," Rex interjected, wishing to keep to the topic of the Dutch real estate developer. "He was telling me about his new nightclub in Marigot. Says it will rival anything in Paris."

"He will make it happen. People will flock to Marigot."

"I suppose The Stiletto was a big attraction when it first opened?"

"I wouldn't know. I have been here less than two years. He tends not to keep his managers very long."

"Why is that?"

"Doesn't like people knowing too much about his business, I guess."

"Is there something shady going on?"

The bar manager stood up and rounded the bar. "Can I get you a soft drink?" he asked, spritzing soda into a glass for himself.

Rex declined. The manager swept an arm around the mirrored walls and chandeliers of the cabaret lounge. "This is just show. His real money is in gemstones. Liquid assets. I was a jeweller back in the Hague. He wears a million dollars on his fingers alone, including a rare and flawless Larimar of pure lagoon blue."

Rex wondered if that was the sapphire he'd seen. "Hence the bodyguard-valet."

"He has many baboons. Oscar. Nito. Sergei. They come and go too. I really cannot tell you anything more."

"I'd just like to see the video proving Mr. Bijou was here so I can exclude him from my inquiry."

The manager shrugged. "Come with me."

Rex followed down a corridor to an office that doubled up as a storeroom. A screen on a wall monitored the front entrance and showed passers-by on the street. With a few strokes of a laptop keyboard, Erik called up time- and date-stamped footage, in black and white, of an immaculately dressed Bijou, followed closely by Oscar, approaching the club just before six the night Sabine disappeared.

"Satisfied?" Erik asked as Bijou's image on screen disappeared beneath the camera on his way through the entrance.

"Can I see him leaving? Just to be sure." Rex still

hoped against hope to rule out the resort guests—and one in particular—as suspects in the Sabine Durand case.

THIRTEEN

The Weeks invited Rex to a cook-out at their cabana on Saturday night. Since David was a cordon bleu chef, the dinner promised to be special, especially as the ingredients were to be purchased fresh from the Marigot market that morning. The couple persuaded Rex to go with them to the French capital, which he had only passed through when he first arrived.

"Marigot's a bit provincial," Toni told him as Pascal drove them across the countryside in the limo.

She wore large sunglasses and a white linen dress that set off her exotic looks, her husband vastly improved in street clothes that hid his skinny legs. When they arrived, Pascal dropped the three of them off, arranging to meet them later at the Café Terrace.

The market, a short walk from the town center, blended a relaxed European feel and Caribbean flair. Tourists and locals bartered with merchants displaying tropical fruit and vegetables beneath bleached canvas canopies. Rice, fresh produce, incense, saffron, and curry powder mingled with the tang of fish and salt air. On the sea front, pelicans dove for scraps from the morning's catch. David wandered off toward the boats to purchase mahi-mahi and shrimp.

Meanwhile, Rex looked for a gift that might appeal to his mother. Circulating the souvenir stalls with Toni, he pictured Moira and her American lover arm-in-arm at an Iraqi market, one that had been subjected to bomb and mortar attacks, which no doubt lent an edge of risk and danger to their romance. He consoled himself that Moira might already regret sending him the letter. Not that he would take her back now. *No, Moira Wilcox, ye made your bed and on it ye shall lie.* He considered instead how refreshing it would be to see Helen again, a lass with a quick sense of humor and down-to-earth good sense—and the sweetest blue eyes. He was glad now of her decision to join the group of teachers from her school on a cruise. Soon she would be steaming toward him at full speed aboard the flagship *Olympia*.

"What about this bird feeder for your mother?" Toni suggested, holding out a hand-carved coconut on a rope.

"Aye, she likes birds, but we live in a Victorian terraced house with only a narrow garden, and I'm not sure a coconut would fit in. She has extremely traditional tastes."

"How about some Magic Spice then? It's what's going on the mahi-mahi tonight. David claims it contains pot."

"Ehm, she does not cook. She's busy with her charities and, to be quite honest, to inflict her cooking on anybody would be an uncharitable act in itself. And our housekeeper would never use anything like that."

"Well, maybe one of these silk shawls with fringes." Toni expertly whipped through the hangers exhibiting a shimmering array of color.

"That would be just the ticket!" Rex selected one that was dyed in sunset hues, knowing it would probably end up adorning a table in one of the guest bedrooms. His mother would appreciate the gesture nonetheless. "I'm glad we got that out of the way," he said, paying for it and taking the bag from the vendor.

"Anyone else you need to shop for?" Toni asked.

"My son. But that's easy. He likes shot glasses for his collection."

David joined them with a large packet of fish, and they meandered through the rest of the market before heading down a boulevard interspersed with modern storefronts flaunting designer brands for everything from perfume to sporty sun visor hats. In this respect, Marigot resembled the cosmopolitan thoroughfares of St. Philipsburg, if not its seedy underbelly. Rex thought back to The Stiletto, where he had seen Bijou on video exiting the club the way he'd come, the bar manager insisting his employer had never left during that time, either by the main entrance or delivery door. It had been disappointing news.

At the wine store, Rex purchased four bottles of the best wine as his contribution to the dinner that night while Toni went off to buy cheese. Then, carrying the groceries between them, they found the limo parked up the side street from the café where Pascal awaited them. As Toni left to fetch him, Rex set the bags down by the trunk of the car.

"David, you knew Sabine from before, when she waited tables at your restaurant..."

"Yes, before I opened the cordon bleu school. She was still a struggling young actress. It was a French restaurant, and her French accent was an asset, plus she knew her wines."

"So you must have got to know her quite well."

"Well enough. Toni worked at the restaurant at the time, and they sometimes didn't see eye to eye, but nothing beyond the usual bickering that goes on in a restaurant. Sabine met our old friends, the Winslows, there and they ended up letting her their basement flat. Eventually, Sabine went on to bigger and better things than waitressing."

"She met Vernon."

"Her star was already set by then, but there's no doubt he made things happen more quickly for her. She was on holiday at La Plage with the Winslows one summer while Vernon was here with his first wife. They ran into each other a few years later in New York. Vernon was divorced by then."

"Elizabeth told me she didn't approve of the match."

David Weeks shrugged his narrow shoulders. "I thought Vernon quite a catch. Rich, lots of connections in the entertainment business, both American and British. But Elizabeth thought the age difference would be a problem."

"Maybe Sabine was looking for a father figure. And Vernon is in great shape for his age."

"Now you mention it, Sabine was estranged from her parents. Her father didn't approve of her acting aspirations. They live in the stuffy *sixième arrondissement* in Paris. Elizabeth and Paul were like surrogate parents to her." David glanced at his watch. "Where did Toni get to?"

At that moment, his wife turned the street corner with Pascal in tow. "Sorry to keep you waiting. I had a quick Porto at the café."

"Nice for *you*," David grumbled peevishly. "We're dying of thirst out here, and the fish will start to ponk."

"David, please don't exaggerate."

"We have cold drinks in da car, don' you worry, Mr. Weeks," the driver intervened with tact, unlocking the doors.

David stared crossly at his wife as she got in the back, but she seemed unruffled. She even winked becomingly at Rex who piled in after her.

"What do you plan to do this afternoon?" she asked as they relaxed into the air-conditioned comfort of the limo headed back to La Plage d'Azur Resort.

David pointedly raided the inbuilt drinks cabinet, offering Rex a choice of wine, beer, or soda.

Rex accepted a diet Coke. "First, I thought I'd explore the far end of the beach for lunch and find a quiet spot to write my postcards."

"Try The Sand Bar," David recommended, happier now that he had a Heineken in hand. "There's a nice shaded spot on the wooden terrace, and the rum drinks are cheap."

"I don't intend to drink too many of those. I want to work on the case this afternoon."

"Well, don't work *too* hard," Toni said. "Tonight's supposed to lighten the mood a bit after what happened."

The inference was that she'd had enough of the gloom surrounding Sabine's disappearance. Clearly, from everything she had said and written on the subject, not much love had been lost between the two women. After helping Pascal and David take the dinner supplies to the Weeks' front door, Rex made a detour to his cabana before setting out for The Sand Bar, equipped with his postcards and notepad, and everything else he might need for a quiet afternoon at the beach. He still had to figure a way to outsmart that fox Bijou, but it was hard to do when the fox was in his own territory and had all the loopholes covered and the police held at bay. The man might not have been directly involved in Sabine's mysterious disappearance, but he had something to hide. Rex was sure of it.

However, by the time he left for the Weeks' barbecue that evening, showered and dressed, he had not made much progress in the case. The potent daiquiri at The Sand Bar, added to the various distractions afforded by the screaming hordes on the banana boat and other water sports in the bay, had not been conducive to achieving a whole lot of productive thinking.

A sea breeze stirred the fronds in the palm trees

along his path, agitating the Chinese lanterns, still unlit. The sobbing wail of a saxophone vibrated through the sultry air, serenading him from a CD player at the Weeks' eighth and last cabana in the row. The guests in pareos and wraps—David in an apron, but not the Male Chauvinist Pig one referred to in his wife's testimony—gathered on the back patio, sipping tall drinks decorated with striped straws and mini paper parasols. Gaby, flaxen hair flowing down her bare back, offered him a plate of pumpernickel squares topped with smoked salmon. As he thanked her in Latin, he spotted Elizabeth Winslow in her flame-colored sarong and the Greek necklace with the interlocking wave motif.

"You're staring at me. I must look especially ravishing tonight," she joked.

"That you do." He led her aside. "There's also something bothering me, that I hope you can help clear up."

"I'll try."

"It concerns a photo of you on Vernon's phone taken the night of Sabine's disappearance."

Elizabeth caught her breath slightly. "At the party? People were taking pictures all night. It was just us, and Hastings didn't object. He must have decided to bend the rules for Paul's birthday. But I honestly can't remember everything. We were all quite blotto."

"But Vernon swears he didn't have his phone on him that night."

"Perhaps someone picked it up by mistake. Is it important?"

"It was later found at the promontory."

"Maybe Vernon dropped it. How do you know you can believe him?"

"I don't." Rex gazed around the festive patio, taking in the guests. How did he know he could believe any of them?

Brooklyn was conspicuous by his absence. Rex inquired after him, not having seen him all day.

"Dropped us like a hot brick," David complained, manipulating the fish fillets on the grill. "Makes me think Sabine was the only reason he hung around in the first place."

"Maybe he's got someone in Philipsburg," Pam said. "That's where he spends most of his time. I haven't seen his cute butt on the beach in over a week."

"He's in mourning for Sabine," Sean O'Sullivan warbled, already four sheets to the wind.

"Will you listen to him prattling on," Nora said to the company at large, eyes flitting toward Vernon who sat morosely in a far corner.

"Brook flew back to the States," Paul Winslow informed everyone. "He'll be back Wednesday."

That was news to Rex.

"He had to put out a fire on Wall Street. Loss of investor confidence in some company or other."

Rex flopped back in his chair.

"Don't look so put out, old chap." Winslow handed him a Guinness. "He said he had to leave in a hurry to avoid a tropical depression that's moving in. I hate to think of that plane of his being buffeted around like a shuttlecock over the ocean. I told him to get going before it was too late."

Rex wondered what incentive Brooklyn could possibly have to return if it was true that Sabine had been his main reason for being at La Plage. Thinking of love interests, he remembered he was meeting Helen off the ship in Philipsburg on Monday and arranged with Winslow for the loan of his Jeep.

"By the way, Paul, do you know of a club down there called The Stiletto?"

"I don't, but Duke might. He knows all the joints in Philipsburg."

The Texan turned toward them, puffing on a fat Cuban cigar. "Do I feel my ears burnin'?"

"Rex was enquiring about The Stiletto on the Dutch side."

"Haven't been in a coupla years, not since that business with one of the dancers getting murdered. Poor kid. They found her body in a cellar."

"Do you remember seeing her at the club?" Rex asked.

"Sure do. Face like an angel, body like a—"

Pam silenced him with a nod toward Gaby, whose mother promptly sent her on an errand.

"What a combination!" Farley stuck the cigar in his mouth.

"Has this anything to do with Monsieur Bijou and our case?" Winslow asked Rex.

"Maybe not with *our* case. Someone I believe to be a reliable source supplied an alibi for Bijou the night Sabine went missing."

"Bijou took me to The Stiletto the first time," the Texan said. "Back when he was looking for investors for his club-casino in Marigot. He was scouting out the best dancers on the island. He bought out The Stiletto at around that time."

"Was he personally acquainted with Leona Couch?"

Duke Farley prodded his malodorous cigar in Rex's direction. "Leona. Yeah, that was her name. He was fascinated by her. When she did her routine, he looked like his borehole had yielded a sh—" Another warning look from Pam. "Load of oil," he finished.

Rex pulled his pipe from his pocket and pensively thumbed Clan tobacco into the bowl. He found he resorted less to the habit in hot weather, but the mellow-sweet fragrance would go some way to counteracting Farley's cigar smoke polluting the storm-expectant air. In deference to the non-smokers crowded around them, he moved away toward Sean O'Sullivan standing by himself on the patio and gazing out to sea, a drink perched on the balustrade. The Irishman had been the first person to link Bijou to the Jewel Killings. Rex was now anxious to probe him for more information before further drink rendered him senseless.

FOURTEEN

When Rex returned to his cabana later that night, he eased open Brooklyn's door and was reassured to see his personal items lying about the room. It wasn't simply that he would feel slighted if Brooklyn had just taken off without saying goodbye; Rex realized when he first heard of his departure that he genuinely liked and admired the man. He was courageous, movie star handsome, and highly successful, and yet for all that, appeared to be someone who lent an ear in time of trouble and extended a hand in time of need.

He sincerely hoped he was not wrong about Brooklyn Chalmers.

The next morning, Rex awoke dehydrated from a slight hangover, the Weeks having plied him with wine and stout at the barbecue, and he found the room darker than usual, even at this advanced hour. Violent wind from a rainstorm had knocked the frond of a coconut palm against the cabana roof all night, and now a blustery day greeted him when he stepped onto the patio in his slippers.

A tornado-shaped cloud loomed on the horizon. The last sailboat had disappeared from the bay to find safer haven. A few remaining yellow umbrellas stood askew and furled on the sand, contributing to the desolate scene. Since it was clearly not beach weather, Rex decided to spend part of the day canvassing the nearby tourist spots, starting with the Sundown Ranch.

"'The Rundown Ranch,' as Sabine and I jokingly called it," Brooklyn had confided the other day when he gave Rex a photo of the two of them standing by a weathered paddock fence.

After the recent storm, the gully-washed road proved more hazardous than usual, and he made slow progress in Winslow's Jeep to the ranch, where Brooklyn's photo of him and Sabine elicited an almost hysterical response from the elderly owner. *Mon Dieu!* She knew Mademoiselle Sabine very well, always personally made sure Dancer was available and fresh for her ride. *Quelle horreur!* To think such an atrocity had happened not three *kilometres* from here! After all, the young woman's dress and bracelet had been found on the beach—something *terrible* must surely have taken place. Now, theft, yes that certainly happened from time to time. Just two weeks ago, the dispensary in the stables had been broken into and some potent drugs stolen. "*Des drogués*," the ranch owner said, throwing up her hands in despair and making her eyes go spacey in imitation of a drug addict. They did not care what they put in their bodies, these people!

She shook her head sorrowfully at the photograph. "*Ah, le pauvre!*" she exclaimed, referring to Brooklyn. The two lovebirds had been so *gais* together. How he must miss her...

Tapping the photo against the palm of his hand, Rex stepped back through the mire in the forecourt to the Jeep. A woman unsaddled a horse steaming from its recent exercise and hosed it down in the yard. As he got into the Jeep, he removed his muddy sandals and placed them upside down on the passenger mat, and drove barefoot out through the broken-down gate, leaving behind the smell of wet hay and manure. He proceeded along Le Galion Beach Road until he came to a large meshed structure with a sign advertising the Butterfly Farm, which he'd been told was really a butterfly sanctuary.

After paying his admission and declining the guided tour, he entered the net enclosure. Enya's melodic voice floated down from the speakers as he ambled through the giant terrarium that harbored hundreds of butterfly species from Saba, Cambodia, Trinidad, Indonesia, China, and other parts of the world, according to his brochure. The colorful winged insects meandering among the flowering plants in the soothing green shade were every bit as exotic in appearance as the places from which they originated. Intricately patterned ones and those with trailing wings glided around him. A Monarch alighted on his shoulder.

"It may be attracted to your aftershave," the guide remarked before turning back to her group of visitors and describing how butterflies mated for up to thirty-six hours out of their two-week lifespan. When the mating was disturbed, they flew away together, the female carrying the male. This drew laughter from the crowd. Rex overheard, too, that the farm had been the brainchild of two eccentric Englishmen, which surprised him less than the oversexed lives of butterflies.

The serene surroundings, refreshingly cool after the rain, exerted a calming influence, and he lingered longer than intended, studying pupae that resembled exquisite earrings and following with his gaze a stately Red Peacock with black markings, a large purple and yellow eyespot on the tip of each wing. Finally, making sure no butterflies had adhered to his clothing or hair—more likely attracted to his shampoo, since he didn't wear aftershave—he exited the screened door and stepped into the souvenir store.

"Can you tell me if you recognize this couple?" he asked the middle-aged woman at the counter, showing her the snapshot of Brooklyn and Sabine.

"Well, I recognize *her*," the surprised store clerk said in a broad English accent. "She's that missing actress, Sabine Duras."

"Durand."

"Are you a reporter?" she asked in a forthright manner.

"No, I'm a friend of a friend hoping to locate her."

"*She* was here, but I don't know the man in your photo—I'd remember such a hunky bloke. Not that the young man with her wasn't attractive too."

Rex's heart raced in excitement. "Do you remember his nationality?"

"They requested a French-speaking guide, but she spoke English with me. She autographed one of our brochures. The photo in the local paper didn't do her justice."

"What did her friend look like?"

"Medium height, thin, dark hair, sexy smile. He wore dark wraparound sunglasses and never took them off, so I didn't get a chance to look at his eyes. He seemed a bit twitchy."

"Twitchy?"

"Sort of nervous. Kept looking around. Maybe he was worried about the paparazzi, but Saint Martin is very low key really and we tend to respect people's privacy here. Not that she's exactly an A-list actress. I mainly recognized her from a mascara advert she did some years ago on British TV. No idea who he was."

"When was it they came in?"

"Two weeks ago, maybe. A Monday, I think. She bought a framed display of a great tiger moth. We only had the one, so I ordered another for the shop." The clerk rolled a finger down a handwritten list on the counter. "Here's the entry. July ninth."

Sabine had vanished the very next day. As Rex headed back toward the resort for lunch, he wondered about this new man. How many men were there in Sabine's life anyway? Was he connected to Bijou?

Pale gray clouds mottled the sky, threatening more rain. His thoughts turned to Helen. Hopefully the weather would clear up by tomorrow in time for her visit. He recalled how they had watched the swans on the partially frozen lake in Sussex and kissed chastely under the mistletoe. They'd exchanged cards and e-mails since Christmas, had spoken a few times on the phone, but there had been a mutually observed reticence in their conversations. He could not be sure if she was still involved with the mathematics teacher at the school where she worked as a student counselor. And, of course, Moira had still been in the picture, so there could be no question of taking the friendship further.

Now that his conscience was clear with regard to Moira Wilcox, he looked forward to Helen's visit as much a mooning teenager on his first date. The butterfly park had put him in a romantic mood.

FIFTEEN

Docked on Great Bay, a white multi-tiered floating hotel dwarfed the tenders ferrying passengers to port. The yellow funnel emblazoned with "Fun-Sun" in blue letters assured Rex this was indeed Helen's ship. But where was she?

Suddenly he spotted her through the crowd milling by the terminal. "Helen!" he shouted, cupping his hands to his mouth and waving frantically.

She ran toward him, a smile breaking out on her face. Her nautical-style white and navy summer dress fit her just right. Her tanned skin brought out the blue in her eyes, and she had done something with her hair—he couldn't tell what, but it seemed fluffier than he remembered.

"You look wonderful," he said, deliberating whether to embrace her, and suddenly wanting to very much.

"And you look very huggable." She stood on her toes in her mid-heel sandals and flung her arms around his shoulders. "Do I get a kiss?"

Gathering her in his arms, he kissed her full on the lips.

"Do you notice anything about me?"

Rex panicked. Such a question from a woman always inspired him with dread. Had she lost weight? "You did something with your hair?" he asked hopefully.

"I'm wearing the earrings!"

"So you are." The tiny turquoise-studded swans he had bought for her in Swanmere Village dangled from her ears.

"I didn't notice them at first because your hair sort of covers them. It looks very nice, by the way. Very soft and wavy."

She smiled, and he felt pleased with himself for making such an adroit comeback.

"Honey-chile," a plump woman called out from a folding chair beside a crate of beads. "Only a dollar a braid." Her own raven tresses were divided into right cornrows—or canerows as they were called in the Caribbean, according to the women guests at the resort, among whom the topic of hair cropped up quite a bit.

"Maybe later," Helen replied wistfully.

Never able to understand the compulsion women had for changing their hairstyles, he took her hand and drew her away. They passed the duty-free shops and discount stores on Front Street where merchants stood at their posts bracing for the onslaught of bargain-seekers let loose from the cruise.

"I can't believe how cheap clothes and electronic

goods are here," Helen exclaimed. "And look at those Gucci watches in the window!"

"Probably knockoff." Rex spotted tortoiseshell compacts like the one he had seen in Nora O'Sullivan's possession. Perhaps Sabine had bought hers here.

Helen stopped to gaze at a display of blue Delft china from Holland.

Rex found a seat inside the store and waited patiently until, holding a small bag of purchases, Helen led him back onto the street.

"Oh, look, the Guavaberry Emporium. I read you can try some for free."

They sampled the sweet liqueur at the counter. Helen opted to buy an opaque green bottle of banana rum instead.

"Can we get lunch now?" Rex asked.

"If we must. All we've been doing on the ship is eating. I think some people go on cruises just for the food, judging by the size of the passengers. But, it is good food."

"I haven't eaten since my *pain au chocolat* this morning."

They settled for an outdoor table at a dockside café where they could watch the boats, and ordered drinks and seafood platters.

"You don't look like you got a lot of sun during your week out here," Helen observed.

"A tan makes my freckles stand out. Anyway, we had rain over the weekend—but it's cleared up nicely." He looked up in appreciation at the cloudless blue sky.

"Are you having a good time?"

"Except for when I have to speak French, which seems to afford much mirth to anyone within earshot."

"Your Scots accent must sound funny in French. I can't wait to hear you speak it."

"Not a chance."

Helen chuckled into her glass of white wine.

"Well, here we are." Rex extended his arms to indicate their Caribbean surroundings. "I do like the island lifestyle."

"I have to say, you're less uptight than when I first met you. And you look totally different in casual clothes."

Rex may have looked casual, but there was nothing casual about the way he had tried on four shirts that morning in an effort to look as appealing as possible for Helen. He had finally decided on a loose-fitting button-down shirt worn over khaki shorts reaching his knees and equipped with so many pockets he was convinced he would forget in which one he'd placed the car keys.

"I bought these clothes in Miami, down to the designer leather flip-flops, which Campbell assured me were worth the extra forty dollars—even though they looked just like the no-name brands to me."

"Campbell has good taste."

"If 'good' equates to 'expensive,' I can assure you he does. When I was a student, the only clothes labels we knew were Wrangler and Levi." Rex sighed with nostalgia. "Life was simpler then, and we managed quite well without mobile phones."

"You old dinosaur."

Helen said it in such a fond way that he suddenly liked the idea of being an old dinosaur. Well, not *old* exactly, but a seasoned. warrior dinosaur. He relaxed in his chair and signaled to the passing waiter for another beer and white wine for Helen.

"Have you heard from your girlfriend yet?" she asked.

"Aye, well, there's been a development."

As they tackled their seafood shells, he told her about Moira's desertion and how he felt like a fool after making all those inquiries over the phone to her lodgings and work, and to the British Embassy in Baghdad. "She could have told me sooner and spared me all the trouble," he concluded.

"She was probably embarrassed."

"As well she should be."

"So do I get to see where you're staying now that you're a free man?"

"If you like. It's at the other end of the island but we can get there in half an hour. I better warn you, though—it's a nudist resort."

"No! Are you having me on? You of all people?"

"I keep my swimming trunks on," Rex said modestly.

Helen wiped a tear of laughter from her eye.

"I'm not as much of a prude as all that, you know. Isn't that what you called me back at Swanmere Manor?"

"I did," Helen said, recovering slowly. "So, do you interview all these people while they're in the never-

never?" She chuckled again.

"Mostly, but it's strange how quickly you get used to it. After a few days, you hardly notice at all."

"Well, I'm jealous. The thought of you ogling naked young women all day..."

"There's no need for jealousy. And most of them aren't that young." He raised his glass. "I only have eyes for you!"

"Flatterer." She mouthed him a kiss across the table. "So how is Campbell getting on in Florida?"

"He finished his first year with a good grade point average."

"Good for him."

Rex thumbed his glass. "It's hard when they move so far away from home, but it's interesting seeing him grow into his own person. And my mother's getting on. I don't know how long she'll be around."

"Rex, you sound lonely!"

"Well, now that Moira's run off, I'm feeling quite abandoned. I'm glad you came, Helen, I truly am."

"It's not just a question of being on the rebound, is it?"

"Definitely not! To tell the truth, I'm glad it turned out this way. I always felt an attraction for you, lass. I really enjoy being with you."

"Likewise—well, you know how I feel about you." Helen tipped the rest of her wine in her mouth and slid her purse strap over her shoulder. "How about a quick foray into the Sint Maarten Museum?"

"What, you mean *now*? I thought you wanted to see where I was staying." And he wanted to spend some personal time with her. He must have looked less than enthused as he hurriedly paid the bill.

"I only have one day here to absorb some of the culture. Did you know, the first settlers here, the Arawaks..."

Rex only half paid attention as he concentrated on finding the museum, which was within walking distance but hidden down an alleyway. The converted nineteenth-century dwelling held an archived collection of sepia photographs of hurricanes ripping through palm trees and structures, and an assortment of musketry, blackened cookware, and other island artifacts in the glass displays.

"Oh, look at these funny misshapen cannon balls," Helen exclaimed.

"Here's a model of the *Fair Rosamund* slave ship." A diagram showed how the captive human cargo was packed like sardines in the hold.

"A disgrace," Helen murmured beside him.

"What now?" he asked hopefully when they had seen everything the small museum had to offer. "My side of the island? The beach there is gorgeous."

"I've seen plenty of beaches. I want to see more of you." She raised an eyebrow in unmistakable wickedness.

Rex cleared his throat. "My chariot awaits."

He escorted her to Paul's beat-up safari-style Jeep and stowed her purchases on the back seat. Pulling out of the parking space, he proceeded to give a potted history of the island, announcing proudly that Philipsburg had been founded in 1763 by John Philips, a Scottish captain in the Dutch navy.

"Those intrepid Scotsmen," Helen said, smiling at him.

He took the most direct route back to the north-east portion of St. Martin, making good time to the resort. Leaving the Jeep outside his cabana, he ushered Helen inside before they could be accosted by a nude guest. He flipped the door sign to "*Do Not Disturb*" and told her his roommate was in New York. "Fortunately for me," he added. "If you met him, you'd forget all about yours truly."

"Now, why would you say that? Is he very good-looking?"

"Extremely. Brooklyn even races cars and flies his own plane."

Helen laughed. "Ah, well. I suppose I'll just have to do with you then, won't I?"

"Thanks very much."

She planted a kiss on his mouth. "This is so airy and tasteful," she said, looking around the spare but comfortable furnishings in the living room. Oh, a beach view!" And then seeing a vase on a table containing a dozen dewy red roses with a note among them, asked, "Are those for me?"

"Of course. Your name's on the card." Per his instructions to the front desk that morning. "I debated bringing flowers to you at the port, but thought they'd just get in the way or else wilt in the car." He hoped she didn't think him presumptuous.

"They smell divine." Helen drew out the tiny envelope in the bouquet, opened it, and read aloud:

"'O my Luve's like a red, red rose
That's newly sprung in June'"

"Robbie Burns," Rex said. "I can recite the whole poem by heart. It's my party piece."

"How very romantic." She clasped her hands around his neck and kissed him. Rex returned the kiss with fervor and pressed her to him. Her fingers moved to his shirt buttons. "I've always wanted to see under a Scotsman's kilt—or shorts," she confessed.

Rex stepped away and swept open the bedroom door with a bow. "I hope I do Bonny Scotland proud."

SIXTEEN

"I wish I could stay here," Helen said stretching beside Rex in the bed. Her face looked as fresh as the roses he had given her, her eyes clear and bright. He felt pretty good himself.

Glancing at the alarm clock, she gave a sigh. "I suppose I'd better get up and take a quick shower."

Rex lazed in bed, listening to the water running in the next room. A pity she had to leave so soon. Already he was looking forward to their next meeting back home—well her home in Derby, where he'd promised to visit one weekend next month.

"Is there any mineral water?" Helen asked, returning to the room wrapped in a towel, and her hair in a turban. "I worked up quite a thirst!"

"Shameless lass," he said throwing off the rumpled covers.

He pulled on his boxers and followed her into the living room, where she walked onto the patio, toweling her hair. The Weeks waved from the beach. Helen gave an enthusiastic wave back.

"Don't encourage them. We don't have much time left to ourselves."

"Who are they?" she asked, taking her cold drink from him.

"David and Toni. They own a cookery school in Richmond." He tapped her pert nose. "We best get going."

A quarter of an hour late, he opened the door of the Jeep, and she slid inside. As he drove toward Philipsburg, he couldn't take his eyes off her tanned knees, covered in a fine down of golden hair.

"How is the case going?" she asked.

"Slowly. It keeps growing tentacles. The evidence conveniently points to the husband, but it's all circumstantial. His phone was found at the scene—that's to say the place from which Sabine Durand vanished, and he was the last person to arrive at the restaurant where the guests were gathered for a birthday party. He suspected his wife of having an affair with my millionaire playboy roommate, and there are witnesses to the husband physically abusing her in the past."

"Even the British tabloids have got hold of this one. They're drawing comparisons between her and that pretty American student, Natalee Holloway, who went missing on Aruba." Helen shook her head sadly.

"Since no body's been found in this case either, the local authorities aren't proceeding further with the investigation, and Sabine's parents don't seem to have kicked up much of a fuss. All I can hope is to get closer to the truth of what happened."

"You solved the case at Swanmere Manor. It makes

sense the new owners of the hotel would have thought of you when their friend disappeared."

Rex shook his head. "I don't know if this case will ever be closed. If sharks got to her, there's little chance of finding her remains and performing an autopsy."

"I have absolute faith in you."

"Thanks for the vote of confidence, but don't jinx it." He checked the map on the dashboard to make sure they were still on the right road.

"Any other suspects?" Helen asked.

"I thought I might be on to something. I went to check out a dance club owned by a certain Monsieur Bijou."

"Mr. Jewel. Is that his real name?"

"Not exactly. He's a Dutch national by the name of Coenraad van Bijhooven."

"No wonder he changed it. What did you find out?"

"Only that he has a solid alibi for the night Sabine went missing, which is more than can be said for most of the guests at the resort. The bar manager at the club has a dated surveillance tape of him parading through the doors in a white suite at five fifty-five the evening in question and leaving at the end of the night."

"Could this Bijou have sent someone to do his dirty work for him?"

"From what an Irish guest at the resort told me, Bijou likes to do his own dirty work. The victims found who may be connected to him were strangled and had semi-precious jewels stuck in their navels. Besides, it would have been hard to conduct an abduction at the beach. The spot is somewhat inaccessible and there's a chance of being heard." Rex thumped the steering wheel in frustration. "There are so many things that don't add up."

"Like what?"

"Sabine was supposedly seeing a chiropractor, but the phone number is bogus. And I couldn't find a Dr. Sganarelle anywhere on the island."

"Another unusual name," Helen said pensively, staring out her window at the passing countryside. "It's a character out of a play by Molière, the seventeenth-century French playwright."

"What sort of character?"

"A miser who doesn't want to part with his daughter's dowry, so he prevents her from having suitors and leaving the house. When she becomes 'lovesick,' her secret admirer pretends to be a doctor so he can see her. I had to study the play for French 'A' level."

"A ruse. Of course!" Rex swerved and brought the Jeep to a standstill on the grass verge.

"Do we have a flat?" Helen asked anxiously.

"Since mobile phones are frowned upon at the resort, it might have been some sort of code to meet—an untraceable call. You truly are a multi-faceted woman," Rex murmured, turning to face her.

"Why, thank you."

"In so many ways," he said, caressing her knee.

"If you hadn't been such a prig, I could have spent a whole week with you here, instead of with a bunch of teachers from my school."

"Is Clive on the cruise?"

"No. And, anyway, I told you I'd finished with

him."

"He's probably sobbing into his logarithms right now." Reaching over the console, Rex slid his hand beneath her dress, and kissed her neck and ear.

"What if someone sees us?"

"There may be a few voyeuristic goats. But they're French goats. I'm sure they've seen it all before." Rex put both hands in her hair and French-kissed her. Suddenly, he felt Helen struggle and push him away. "What's the matter?" he asked in alarm.

"My earring!" she said, feeling her left lobe. "It fell out." She checked in her hair and down the front of her dress, then twisted in her seat, searching frantically around her. "I love these earrings!"

Rex undid his seat belt and bent over to search the mat at her feet, vaguely aware of the sound of a car engine dropping to second gear as it negotiated the road up the hill. He prodded around on the floor and patted around Helen's seat, raising her hemline to make sure the earring hadn't fallen into the lower half of her dress. He heard a tap at his window. Panting from the exertion of being bent double and perspiring slightly, he struggled back into his seat while Helen demurely straightened her dress. Lieutenant Latour's mustachioed face leered through the glass. Rex lowered it.

"Ah, Monsieur Graves. Quelle coincidence! Vous êtes en panne?"

"En what?"

"Vous avez besoin d'aide?"

No, we don't need your blasted help. "Merci, voozette gentee mais nous sommes trez bien," Rex gushed, reassuring him they were fine.

"*Ça se voit!*" the officer said with a glint in his eye.

"It's not what you think!" Even though Helen made him feel like a teenager, it didn't mean he would act like one.

"*Nous étions en panne,*" Helen interjected. "*Mais nous avons reussi a changer le pneu. Quelle chaleur!*" she said, wiping her brow as if from the exertion of having just changed a tire. The swan earring fell out of her hair just then and in her haste to catch it, she knocked it into her cleavage.

"*Madame parle très bien le français!*" Latour complimented her on her French. He winked at Rex and twiddled his mustache. "*Elle est charmante!*"

"Noo sommes en retard por le bateau. Le grand bateau. Ship!" Rex pointed to his watch. "Au revoir. Merci!" He thrust the jeep into gear and tore off down the road with a squeal of tires, from the rearview mirror watching Latour get back in his police car.

"What was all that about?" Helen asked, hooking the silver swan back in her ear.

"He's the gendarme I've been liaising with in the Sabine Durand case."

Helen gave a hoot of laughter. "Of all the cars on all the roads on Saint Martin, he walks up to mine?"

"Something like that. Still, it's not a very big island." Rex groaned. "If I had any credibility to begin with, I've lost it now."

Helen started giggling. I was a good few minutes before she regained control of herself. "Your—your French," she gasped. "It's dreadful!"

"I did warn you." Thanks for coming up with the story of the car braking down. Not that I think he believed us for a minute."

"He seemed quite *gallant* though."

"I'd like to have wiped that smirk off his face. Mind you," Rex said thoughtfully, remembering Latour leaving the house in Grand Case with his own clothes in a state of disarray, "I don't think he's in any position to cast stones."

Although he resented the intrusion and Latour for reading more into his romantic interlude with Helen than there actually was, the episode grew increasingly funny as they embellished it on the way to Philipsburg. Once there, he had difficulty finding a parking space among the taxis depositing passengers. Shiploads of marauding tourists inundated the narrow street of the port, making last-minute purchases. Wives loaded beleaguered husbands with electronic devices, apparel, and all sorts of condiments and ornaments."

"Here, luv, can you manage this lot?" said one. "We still have to get rum for Kevin and some of that Dutch china for Tracy."

Helen hailed a fellow passenger. "Laura! Could you take our picture? Rex, this is a history teacher from my school." She handed the woman her phone and stood against Rex, who draped his arm round her waist while other cruise line passengers and crew jostled past on their way to the terminal. Helen thanked Laura and checked the photo, clearly pleased. "Wait a sec and I'll help you with those bags."

Her friend stood by while Helen and Rex embraced goodbye.

"I'll send you a postcard from Saint Kitts," Helen promised.

Rex in turn proclaimed:

"'And fare thee weel, my only Luve!
And fare thee weel a while!
And I will come again, my Luve,
Tho' it ware ten thousand mile!'"

Helen gave him a final passionate kiss. "The rest of the cruise will pale in comparison with the time spent with you."

"Aye, it was grand, wasn't it?" He released her reluctantly.

The friend smiled sympathetically at Rex and gave one of her bags of souvenirs to Helen to carry. They moved away, Helen glancing back over her shoulder before finally disappearing among the throng of embarking passengers.

This parting was less painful than the last one, Rex reflected. There would be other times, he felt sure of that now. He would call her as soon as he returned to Edinburgh. Consoled by that thought, he went to check there was enough money in the meter. By the time he returned, only a spatter of people remained on the dock.

Helen, a blur behind the white deck rail of her gigantic cruise ship, waved and pointed at him to two women who stood beside her. As he waved her off into the fading sun, he thought how the Full Moon Party at the end of the month would have made for a truly special occasion with Helen.

He hoped to have solved the case by then—and she may have given him a clue.

SEVENTEEN

"Who's the petite blonde I saw you with yesterday?" David Weeks asked as they crossed on the path leading from the resort lobby to the cabanas.

"A friend from home." Rex didn't want him to think she was a woman he had casually picked up on the beach. "She came over on a cruise."

"When are we going to meet her?"

"She had to leave with the ship." Although Rex recalled with tenderness how she'd said it could leave without her for all she cared.

"Pity. We could use some new blood in the group. Tensions are running high. All the stress over Sabine, I suppose. Anyway, it's not the same." Weeks glanced at the paper bag in Rex's hand. "I see you got yourself some breakfast. I was just on my way for French pastries myself." His tanned backside retreated up the path.

Rex had become accustomed to nudity on the beach, but it still struck him as strange that the guests wandered into the onsite store to buy groceries with not so much as a stitch on their bodies.

"Rex! Rex!" a Germanic male voice halted him from the parking lot.

He turned mid-stride and saw the Austrian doctor and his family descend from the limousine, Pascal holding the car door open for them.

"My daughter needs to speak with you most urgently."

Rex approached her. "What is it, Gaby?"

She handed him a photo from a packet of processed film. "Who do you think that is?" she asked hesitantly.

"You don't have a camera on your phone?" he asked in mild surprise.

"My parents won't allow me a smartphone yet, just a regular mobile phone."

Very wise, Rex thought. Gaby was only sixteen. He studied the photo carefully.

"Well?" she asked, almost hopping up and down now in excitement.

"It *looks* like Sabine Durand, judging by other photos I've seen of her. Though it's a wee bit difficult to tell for sure because of the sunglasses and wide-brimmed hat."

"They are her blue Christian Dior glasses," Frau von Mueller said, joining them. "I said to Sabine one time how nice they were."

Rex failed to understand why they were showing him a snapshot of the actress when he already knew what she looked like.

"I took it yesterday," Gaby informed him.

"Ah. I see..." But how was that possible, unless...? "Where?" he asked.

"On Saint Barthélemy!" the mother garbled excitedly. "Gaby went to buy a snorkel mask. She heard the voice of Sabine at the café next to the shop *und* she snapped the picture."

"I was not sure at first," Gaby took over, "because—well, I thought she was dead. I was able to take this picture without her seeing me. It was an outdoor café. I had the pictures developed in town and went to pick them up just now."

"It is Sabine," Dr. von Mueller insisted, approaching. "I would know the nose anywhere, even from a photograph. I made it!"

"Who else knows about this?" Rex asked the family, trying to curb his own excitement.

"No one," Gaby said. "First I wanted to be sure and examine the photograph. Here is the address of the dive shop," she added, giving him the receipt from the purchase of her mask.

"She is going to be a fine lawyer, *nein?*" von Mueller said proudly.

Rex smiled at her. "She certainly is."

The girl blushed to her flaxen roots.

"May I keep this photo for the moment?" Rex checked his watch and flagged down the limo, automatically patting down the pockets of his shorts to make sure he had his wallet on him. "Not a word to anyone!" he called back to the von Muellers, putting a finger to his lips.

Pascal rolled down the window. "Yessir, Mr.

Graves?"

"I need to get to Oyster Pond by nine o'clock." Having originally checked the Irvings' alibi for the day Sabine disappeared, he knew a ferry left for St. Barts at that time.

"Hop in."

Rex tore around the sleek black hood of the limousine and settled in beside the driver. "Fast as you can," he instructed. "I'll make it worth your while."

Pascal handled the stretch limo like a race car pro as vehicles and pedestrians prudently leaped out of his path. Rex offered him one of his croissants and stuffed the other into his mouth, leaving buttery flakes on his shirt. He compared his watch to the clock on the dashboard, and calculated how many kilometers they could cover in the minutes left to reach their destination before the ferry sailed away without him. Sensing his anxiety, Pascal floored the accelerator along a clear length of road.

At Oyster Point, dock-hands were already casting off the lines of the large twin-hulled ferry. Rex waved frantically, thrust his fare and his I.D. at the woman behind the kiosk, and jumped aboard.

Thankful he'd had some breakfast to help settle his stomach, he stood on the top deck while the high-speed catamaran set motor sail over a choppy sea. He hoped this island-hopping business wouldn't turn out to be a wild goose chase. Feeling his stomach begin to churn, he took deep gulps of sea air and stared straight ahead at the gray-green mirage of St. Barts to the southwest. The memory of the slave vessel slipping away from the island sprang to mind as the coast of St. Martin receded. Now that Sabine had possibly been spotted, he wondered if she'd acted out an affair with Brooklyn to give her husband a motive for murder, and then made her exit by sea. Had she planted Vernon's phone on the beach to further frame him? If so, why was Elizabeth Winslow on camera? Rex was in no doubt whose face it was in the frame. The outline of the necklace she always wore was unmistakable. Had she aided and abetted Sabine in her plan? Why then had she and her husband brought him to St. Martin to investigate the young woman's disappearance?

Rex found himself impatient to get ashore and on with his inquiries. Already the sun bounced blindingly off the water. He found his sunglasses in one pocket and a stick of sunscreen in another, and smeared the lotion over his face and around the back of his neck. His phone, however, he'd left at his cabana when he went to get breakfast. In his rush to leave the resort with Pascal, he'd forgotten all about it, which could prove a huge inconvenience.

The deck hand served plastic cups of guava juice to the thirty or so passengers, and Rex downed one thirstily. St. Barts grew progressively clearer in focus. He had until four-thirty to find the elusive actress. That was when the catamaran left for Oyster Pond. But the island of St. Barts was no more than ten square miles. How many hotels could be on it? He could enlist the help of the local gendarmes. But what if they were all as mockingly unhelpful as Lieutenant Latour? And Sabine, if indeed alive, hadn't committed a crime. She may even have had good reason to get away from her husband.

A family of tourists pointed overboard in excitement to where a green sea turtle paddled alongside the vessel. Soon after, Gustavia Harbour came into view, a small port bristling with masts from the fleet of fishing and leisure craft. A red-roofed town grew up around the port, off-shooting into the hills.

Rex figured he would need transportation. A rental car would take too long to arrange. Once on dry land, he inquired instead after a moped, the store clerk assuring him it would indeed be able to convey a man of his bulk up the steep inclines of the island. While at the store, Rex picked up a booklet of local restaurants, hotels, and bed and breakfasts, and told the clerk he would be back for the moped.

His day would entail a systematic search of St. Barts, showing the proprietors the photograph of Sabine and, hopefully, tracking her or her lookalike down. He prepared himself for disappointment. After all, the Austrian cosmetic surgeon had seen only a photo of Sabine at the café, and that was with her wearing sunglasses. But if he managed to locate the French actress, he could return to St. Martin and tell the guests at La Plage d'Azur Resort that she was alive and well, and had decided to leave her husband for whatever reason —and then he could fly back to Scotland, case closed.

The obvious place to start was at the café by the dive store printed on Gaby's receipt. "Did you see this woman in here yesterday?" he asked the handsome bartender in his best bad French.

"Yes," the Frenchman answered in English. "She was sitting on the terrace with a man. They ordered the best champagne." He rubbed his thumb and forefinger together. "Big spenders, big tippers."

"Do you happen to know where they're staying."

The bartender turned suddenly cautious. "Why should I tell you, *monsieur?*"

Calculating how big a tip the couple might have left him, Rex slid a twenty-dollar bill across the counter.

The bartender slipped it into his jar labeled "*Pourboires*" as though it were pocket change.

"Well?" Rex prompted.

"I heard them mention l'Auberge Fleurie." The man shrugged with a self-deprecating smile. "I always listen to what a beautiful woman is saying, in case I want to find her again. She briefly took off her sunglasses. Her eyes were the colour of the sea. *Tenez,*" he said gesturing toward the Caribbean stretched out in the sunshine beyond the bay.

"Aquamarine," Rex murmured to himself. It sounded like Sabine all right. "And she was French?" he asked.

The bartender placed a glass of iced water in front of Rex on the counter. "They both spoke perfect French."

"Where can I find the inn?"

"Listen, *monsieur.* What exactly is your business with this woman? *Un moment, s'il vous plaît,*" he called down the bar to a customer, indicting with a forefinger he would be just a minute.

"She left a grieving husband on Saint Martin," Rex replied. "I'm a private detective hired to make sure she has come to no harm."

The bartender looked uncomfortable. "I'm not sure I should give the lovers' secret away."

Rex's jaw muscles flexed in vexation. He didn't have enough twenty-dollar bills to spare and wasn't about to divest himself of his precious British currency. "The location of the inn, if you please. I have the phone number here in this booklet," he said finding it. "It gives the street address, but it would save me valuable time if you could simply point me in the right direction." When the bartender still hesitated, Rex asked for the use of a phone.

The young man gave a shrug of capitulation. "Up on the hill overlooking Grand Saline Beach. But, er, what is a private detective doing without his own phone, *hein?*"

"Long story." Rex downed the water in one go. "Mercy buckets," he said jovially, depositing the glass and pulling away from the bar. He had struck gold!

He returned to the moped rental store, confirmed the directions to the inn, and took off up a rocky hillside, rejoicing in the view of an isolated white sand beach enlacing a turquoise sea. As the road steepened, the feeble motor whined and sputtered in protest. On several occasions it almost expired. Rex ended up abandoning it halfway up the slope among the cacti and wild bougainvillea to retrieve later. Thankful for the sea breezes, he walked the rest of the way and turned into the short gravel driveway to the hotel.

True to its name, the white facade of the inn nestled in a bower of exotic flowers and tropical trees in bloom, the green shutters open to a larger beach sparkling far below the cliff. He mounted the stone steps and entered a hallway. At the reception desk, he paused for breath beneath a whirling ceiling fan and let the air cool his face.

"I'm looking for Mademoiselle Durand," he told the smiling *patronne*, abandoning his French altogether.

"*Ecossais*?"

"Aye, Scottish. Well spotted."

"*Sean Connery est mon James Bond favori.*" The pretty middle-aged woman put a hand to her ample bosom in a coquettish gesture of adoration.

"He's my favourite Bond too. You canna beat a Scotsman, eh?"

The woman responded with a tinkle of laughter. "*Ah, la chose est sûre, monsieur,*" she agreed.

"Och, aye–I was asking aboot Mademoiselle Sabine Durand. Young French lady," Rex said, continuing to exaggerate his Scots slightly. "She's a friend of mine from Saint Martin. I understand she's staying here with her male companion."

"Durand?" The woman shook her head. "I have no one by that name in my book."

Blast! Rex thought, realizing the bartender might have lied about her whereabouts. In which case, he would return to the café and demand his money back with interest—and throw cold water back in his face. "She may have been staying under her friend's name," he said hopefully. "I forget what it is. He's French too."

Rex frowned in feigned frustration. "I must be getting senile."

"You must mean Vernet. A charming couple. *Tout à fait charmant*. And she—*oh là là! Ravissante!* I put them in *la Lune de miel*."

The honeymoon suite—very nice, Rex thought with irony.

"But you are too late, *monsieur*. They checked out earlier this morning."

"Do you know where they went?"

"I only know they sailed away on their boat."

Their boat! Sabine could be almost anywhere in the Caribbean by now, depending on its size. Rex made his disconsolate way down the hill and pulled his moped from out behind the flowering bush where he'd hidden it. Putting it in neutral, he freewheeled down the road into town. With no further use for the moped, he dropped it off at the rental store and found a vacant table under the striped awning of a bistro across from the sleepy harbor. Many of the stores and businesses were closing for lunch. Consulting the menu, he ordered a beer and *steak-frites*. To heck with his diet, he thought; he needed fuel, and fast.

First, though, he should put Vernon Powell out of his misery and let him know his wife was alive. He went inside to locate a phone, missing again the convenience of his cell, for which he'd even gone to the trouble of organizing overseas service. Having first asked his server for the St. Martin code, he slid his credit card into the pay phone and pressed the buttons.

"La Plage d'Azur Resort. Greg Hastings speaking."

"Rex Graves here. I need to speak with Mr. Powell. Can someone bring him to the phone? I'm calling from Saint Barts on an important matter."

"One minute, Mr. Graves." The manager spoke to someone at the desk. "Danielle is going across there right now with the message. You best give me the number you're calling from." Rex read it out to him. "Okay, got it. We'll get back to you in a tick."

Rex watched as his beer passed by on a tray and went after it. "Hold the *steak-frites*," he told the server. "I'm waiting for a call."

As it turned out, he could have eaten his steak and fries plus dessert in the time it took for the call to come through. Fortunately, no one else seemed interested in using the phone. Sensibly, they all had their own phones.

"There is a problem," Hastings informed him as soon as Rex answered.

What now? Rex asked himself.

"Dr. von Mueller is attending to Mr. Powell as we speak." The resort manager paused. Coughed. "He appears to be dead."

"Dead? How?"

"Looks like an overdose. Mr. Chalmers is here and would like to speak to you. I'll pass you on."

"Brook?" Rex asked in surprise. "You're already back from New York!"

"I met with the shareholders Monday morning and got them under control, and flew back out as soon as I could. Rough news about Vernon. Anything I can do?"

"Well, for a start I need to get off this island. Pronto."

"You got it. Greg told me you're on Saint Barts? See you there at the airfield in one hour."

Rex wolfed down his lunch, drained the rest of his beer, and rushed off to find the harbor master before flying out of the island.

EIGHTEEN

Rex was sure the von Muellers, who were so correct and upstanding, would not tell anybody about the sighting of the actress before he returned to the resort. Now that Vernon was dead, he thought it all the more prudent to withhold news of Sabine. However, as Brooklyn's plane bowled down the mountainside runway, he decided he ought to tell the young man who'd clearly been in love with her that she was alive. He waited until they had cleared the airfield and were on their flight path to St. Martin, but Brooklyn spoke first, communicating through their headphones and mics.

"The tower warned we might run into weather." He checked the altimeter reading. "You could have been stranded on Saint Barts."

Even as he spoke, the wind whipped up the waves below them, crumpling the blue tapestry of the sea until it became barely possible to make out the few boats bobbing about like corks on the surface. Rex wondered if Sabine's catamaran was among them, or whether its occupants were far away from the island by now. The harbor master had informed him the *Moonsplash,* captained by a young Frenchman called Jean-Luc Valquez—not Vernet, but fitting the description given to Rex at the Butterfly Farm—had been moored on and off in Gustavia Harbour for several days.

The first few raindrops had fallen when Brooklyn was fueling the Malibu Piper at the St. Barts airfield, water beading down the white fuselage girded with a slim red stripe. Now the wipers worked at a furious pace to repel the deluge. Rex hoped the turbulence wouldn't become too bad. He'd hate to lose his lunch in the plush, air-conditioned six-seater aircraft. He reassured himself it was only a short distance to Grand Case. Brooklyn looked unconcerned by the rainstorm. All the same, he thought it better not to distract the pilot with the news of Sabine until they landed. "What was going on at the Plage when you left?" he asked instead, anxious to hear details of Vernon's death and knowing Brooklyn would not be mourning the loss of her husband too much.

"Pandemonium. Hastings was doing a good job of keeping a stiff upper lip and following proper protocol. The ambulance arrived as I left. And there was a tall gendarme with a twirly mustache waving his arms in the air, like he was directing traffic."

"Lieutenant Latour."

"Hopefully the situation will have calmed down by the time we get back." Brooklyn made adjustments to the controls as the plane began juddering from side to side and rain sheeted down the cockpit windshield. "We'd better climb out of this bad patch and see if we can't give you a smoother ride."

Minutes later they flew out of the angry pile of clouds and Rex could see a smudge of land far below them again. "You think it was suicide?" he asked, unclenching his buttocks and returning to the subject of Vernon.

"No. Accidental maybe. Vernon just wasn't the type to kill himself."

Brooklyn went on to describe the scene at Vernon's cabana as Danielle had recounted it to him. She'd had to use the master key to finally gain access, as the living room sliders were locked too. The last track on the CD was playing the Bee Gees—"Nights on Broadway"—when she walked in. No sign of a struggle. Everything in its place, down to the re-corked bottle of rum and the pair of tumblers rinsed clean on the draining board next to the sink. She found Vernon lying on his bed with his arms folded across his chest, naked as a jaybird, a whiff of rum discernible on his pale lips. But no pills in evidence.

A peaceful scene, Rex acknowledged to himself. But where was the medication or empty container if Vernon had overdosed.

Approaching the coast, Brooklyn spoke into the radio seeking clearance to land. As he guided the plane through driving rain over misty hills and hidden valleys, Rex's throat lodged in his mouth in anticipation of landing. Blurry lights marking the airstrip rushed up to meet them. *Here we go*, he thought, his body tensing. The runway looked terrifyingly short.

The plane swooped down, swaying slightly in the wind, but Brooklyn held course. The landing gear bumped on the tarmac and they hurtled to a controlled stop within a few feet of the barrier. Rex exhaled slowly.

"I'm gonna taxi into that hangar," Brooklyn said. "Pascal should be waiting for us in the parking lot. We made it just in time. The rain's getting worse if that's possible."

The gale blew so strongly that Rex could barely open the cockpit door. By the time he got to the lino he was drenched through. Pascal, dressed in his chauffeur uniform, slid open the driver partition and pointed to a decanter of brandy in the drinks compartment. He had even brought towels. A gust hurled Brooklyn inside ten minutes later.

Rex poured a tumbler of brandy for his roommate as the car splashed through the rain. "All this flying must be a lot of wear and tear on your plane." Not to mention his own nerves, Rex thought, deciding that private air travel wasn't for him.

"The PA-46 is build for long haul," Brooklyn said. "She has a range of one thousand, three hundred and forty-five nautical miles. It's one thousand NMs northwest by west to Fort Lauderdale where I refuel, then almost another thousand to New York, but she can handle it. Flying your own plane is the only way to go."

"Aye, it's very handy," Rex fudged. "Listen, I have news about Sabine I've been waiting to tell you."

"You found her body?"

"Quite the contrary. I have reason to believe she's alive. Gaby von Mueller spotted her on Saint Barts yesterday. That's what I was doing over there."

Brooklyn stared into his brandy glass, clearly more affected by this revelation than flying through hazardous weather conditions. In the ensuing silence, filled only by rain pelting the limo as its tires swished along the wet road, Pascal turned around to face them.

"Don' mean to eavesdrop," he said before diverting his attention back to the windshield, his eyes peering at them in the rearview mirror, "but how come she alive when we all thought she be dead?"

"That's something I still need to find out," Rex said. "I tracked her down to an inn where she was staying with a young Frenchman, who may be the one she was with when she visited the Butterfly Farm."

"You have been busy." Brooklyn studied his glass some more, a frown furrowing his brow. "I can't think of any Frenchmen she hung out with here on the island. I know one who sometimes moors his yacht in the bay off the Plage, but I'm not sure they're acquainted, and he's not her type."

"What is her type?"

Brooklyn sat back in the white leather seat. "Pretty-boys, judging by the servers she flirted with. I didn't think she was serious about anybody."

"Except you?"

"Perhaps. Alive, huh?" Brooklyn looked like a dazed boxer rising in the ring at the last count.

"Did you ever meet her chiropractor, a Dr. Sganarelle?"

"No, but I knew she was seeing one in Philipsburg for her back?"

"Aye well, I think she was getting more than a spinal manipulation."

"You mean she was sleeping with a quack?"

"I doubt he's a chiropractor at all. If it's the same man, he was registered under the name of Vernet at the inn on Saint Barts."

Brooklyn shook his head. "Doesn't ring a bell. Vernet—Vernon. Interesting."

"If it's an assumed name, it may be a subconscious choice. The harbor master on Saint Barts knew him as Jean-Luc Valquez, unless it was someone else."

"Don't know that name either."

The limo pulled through the gate to the resort and deposited them in front of their cabana. No sooner had Rex scrambled into dry clothes than a knock sounded at the door and Greg Hastings stepped inside, propping his dripping golf umbrella against the wall by the mat.

"Thought I'd come over and fill you in on some rather interesting developments. I haven't had a chance yet to speak to the gendarmes about them."

Rex ushered the manager into the living room.

"When you called from Saint Barts and I sent Danielle to fetch Mr. Powell for you, the door to his cabana was locked. Nobody had seen him all day. Sensing something was wrong, she used the office key to get in and found him on the bed. His eyes were wide open and he wasn't breathing. She ran back to reception and I escorted Dr. Von Mueller to the cabana, where he pronounced Vernon Powell dead. A CD was still playing when Danielle found him, so he couldn't have been dead long."

Unless someone else reset the CD player to confuse the police, Rex hypothesized to himself. "Brook told me what Danielle found. It seems odd that a man who was about to take his life would think to rinse out the glass he used to wash down the pills. If there were pills involved. And the presence of a second glass is interesting."

Hastings shrugged. "It's not clear how he died, but when I returned to the main building after taking Dr. von Mueller to number two, one of the cleaning staff told me she'd seen Sabine Durand there not long before Danielle found the body."

The manager's account confirmed Rex's suspicions.

"The gendarme is here," Brooklyn informed them.

Lieutenant Latour strutted into the living room. "*Quel sale temps!*" he exclaimed, sweeping the kepi from his head and brushing water off his waterproof cape.

"Foul weather indeed," said Rex. "Mr. Hastings was just telling me we might have a suspect in Vernon Powell's murder."

"*Encore?* Why must he be murdered? Why must everybody be murdered?" Red blotches appeared on the gendarme's face. "Why not an accidental leetle overdose, *hein?* A straightforward heart attack? Ah, you Sherlock Holmes types! Can you not enjoy our beautiful island without seeing murder under every palm tree? Well, we will know from ze autopsy what happened."

"We dinna have time!" Rex exploded in Scots. "Mr. Powell's wife was here."

"Mademoiselle Durand? *Sans blague!*"

"No joke. Mr. Hastings just found out from a member of staff. Is it not a wee bit suspicious that Sabine Durand stages her death, mysteriously reappears two weeks later, and within an hour her husband is found apparently O.D.'d in his bed, during which time she mysteriously vanishes again? Or would have, had she not been spotted."

"Clementine Guillaume from maid service came forward," the manager explained to Latour. "Ms. Durand swore her to secrecy with a bribe of one thousand euros when she realized the maid had seen her leaving the number two cabana."

"I will need to speak with zis maid. And do we know where Mademoiselle Durand is now?" Lieutenant Latour looked around the living room as though she might be hiding in a corner.

"According to Clementine, she slipped away in the rain dressed in a plastic poncho," Hastings replied.

Brooklyn handed Rex a pair of binoculars. "If she didn't have a getaway car, my guess is she's on one of the cats out there waiting for the storm to abate so she can escape." He led Rex to the open sliders.

Rex adjusted the binoculars and focused on a catamaran at anchor in the middle of the bay. A dinghy was tied to it. The sea chop obscured the name of the craft, but he watched just long enough to decipher some of the letters. A couple of blurry figures scurried about on deck as though preparing the catamaran for sail.

"She's on that boat," he told Brooklyn, holding the glasses steady so his roommate could see. "The *Moonsplash*. That's how she got here from Saint Barts. That's how she left in the first place. The tide was out that night and she swam the short distance to the catamaran, first planting a bloody, torn-off piece of her pareo and her ankle bracelet on the beach."

Sabine would have known from horseback riding along Galion Beach where the tide would be at any given point in the day. She had no doubt picked the evening of Paul Winslow's birthday to disappear, knowing the guests would be in their cabanas getting ready for dinner.

"They're on the move," Brooklyn said in a panic, following the catamaran with his binoculars.

"Lieutenant Latour, can you send a police boat?" Rex asked.

"There's not enough time," Brooklyn interrupted. "The cat could hide out on any number of islands. We need to pick them up before they can get away."

"What if the police launched a chopper?" Hastings suggested.

"*Mais, non, voyons—*"

"Not in this weather," Brooklyn said. "C'mon, Rex, let's go after her."

"How?"

His roommate laughed as though he had just dreamed up a good prank. "I have a key to one of the yachts in the bay. It belongs to that elderly Frenchman I told you about. He's letting me use it while he's away. Get something waterproof on. I'll find Pascal. He knows all about boats. Meet you on the beach in five minutes."

"I don't have anything waterproof," Rex called after him.

"You can take my golf umbrella," said Hastings. "But it might blow inside out in this gale."

"*Tenez.*" Latour shrugged out of his slicker and handed it to Rex. Clearly, he had no intention of going with them. After a brief hesitation, he offered his kepi.

"Thanks, but just the cape. I don't want anyone thinking I'm impersonating a policeman."

Rex couldn't believe he was actually going out on a boat in this weather. The plane ride had been bad enough. But he couldn't let Sabine get away. Again.

NINETEEN

Rex ran to the beach. Peering through the rain, he saw that the Moonsplash had not made much progress and seemed to be in difficulty. Pascal and Brooklyn appeared farther down the wet sand.

"Hop into this old bucket," Brooklyn called to Rex, pointing to a small boat with an outboard motor. "We'll go after them in the *Belle Dame*. Even if Sabine sees us get on the yacht, she'll think it's the owner and crew."

Wading into the water, Rex climbed aboard and sat huddled on a wooden bench seat while rain pelted his slicker. Brooklyn pulled up anchor, and the boat plowed forward as fast as the little coffee mill of an engine could transport the three of them against the roll of the waves.

Pascal, hand on the tiller, wore a fisherman's knit sweater and hood, which Rex assumed he kept in the trunk of his car when he came to work. The hum of the motor was barely audible above the deafening roar of the sea. The rocking motion unsettled Rex's stomach and, after surviving the plane trip, he finally lost his *steak-frites* over the side of the boat. Brooklyn and Pascal appeared too busy with the task of steering and bucketing out water from the bottom of the boat to notice. Rex held his face up to the rain and rinsed out the sour taste in his mouth. With any luck, the yacht would be steadier.

"They'd be crazy to take that twenty-four footer into open water in a storm like this," Brooklyn remarked, his eyes trained on the catamaran which, after some initial floundering, was making progress toward the mouth of the bay.

"Do you know much about yachts?" Rex asked apprehensively.

"I used to race cigarette boats."

"Is there anything you canna do?"

Brooklyn seemed to give the question due consideration. "I can't make an omelet," he answered, and grinned as rain poured down his face.

Pascal nosed the dinghy behind the *Belle Dame*. Concentrating on maintaining his balance, Rex followed Brooklyn up the fiberglass steps at the stern, across a slippery teak sundeck, and up a steep stairway to the pilothouse. Even at this high vantage point, spray lashed against the wraparound tempered glass windows. The yacht dipped and reared like a horse on a carousel. Brooklyn hollered down to Pascal and turned the ignition key. The twin engines leaped to life with a tremendous roar. Added to the swaying motion, the smell of diesel made Rex nauseous, but little remained in his stomach to throw up this time.

As they left the relative shelter of the bay, pushing out past the island to starboard, the heaving of the sea sucked at the hull, the waves around them roiling masses of foam. Rex felt uncomfortable simply watching disasters at sea on television from the comfort of his recliner. Would he were back home now!

Pascal, who had taken over at the helm, fought with the wheel in pursuit of the *Moonsplash*, which was outstripping them at forty-five knots on a course toward Ilet Pinel, the islet near where the rest of Sabine's pareo had been recovered. From time to time, the catamaran disappeared from view amid twelve-foot cliffs of gray water. Distantly visible on shore, the slim palm trees bent sideways in the wind.

"Is this a hurricane?" Rex yelled out to Brooklyn.

"Just a squall. Don't worry, just don't go overboard."

"No chance," Rex said holding onto the console bar with white knuckles. "Can we catch up with them?"

"This is a more powerful boat and Pascal knows these waters. Why don't you go down to the cabin? I'll call when we get near."

"That's okay," Rex said valiantly. How could he ever relate this adventure to Campbell if he had to tell him he'd been cowering below and throwing up in the head? At least up here, he was in the fresh air—and plenty of it.

Water swept over the bow, splashing the glass. A boat out on the ocean was struggling to get its sails down. Pascal called the national police and alerted them to a possible emergency. "Gale force winds up to ninety kilometres an hour off La Plage d'Azur. Sailboat in distress.," he reported, reading out her GPS location.

"Squall, my Scottish foot!" Rex rebuked Brooklyn.

The police boat was already on another call, Pascal relayed to them. All search and rescue boats were busy scooping up fishing vessels and yachts caught in the storm. He tuned in to the local VHF frequency, and they heard the crackling SOS from the sailboat. "Mayday! ... Mayday!," called an American voice. "We're taking on water."

Pascal turned to Rex and Brooklyn. "Do we go pick dem up?"

"Their mast could snap if we don't," Brooklyn said. "They could end up on the rocks."

Rex thought quickly. He couldn't let a murderess get away, but nor could they leave the sailboat and crew to their fate. "Aye, we'd better save that boat," he agreed.

Brooklyn nodded. "If we can tow them into the head of the bay, we can still go after the catamaran."

Suddenly, Pascal pointed. Rex stood on his toes to see over an intervening ridge of waves. The *Moonsplash* had capsized. Two figures bobbed about in the water in life preservers.

"Them first," he told Pascal. "Before sharks get to them or they drown."

Within fifteen minutes, Rex and Brooklyn had hoisted the couple out of the water onto the deck. Not a word was spoken between Brooklyn and Sabine. Rex explained who he was and why he was chasing them. The bedraggled and shivering young man with Sabine looked about him like a caged animal.

"I'll take them below," Rex told Brooklyn, whose attention was now back on the lurching sailboat. "Can you get it to shore?"

"Aye, aye, skipper." Brooklyn, intent on the rescue, refused to meet Sabine's eyes.

"Here, take these life vests in case Ms. Durand and her friend get any ideas about making a swim for it."

Sabine cast Rex a look of disdain. She had the beguiling eyes of a cat, though he couldn't tell if they were more green or more blue. Duke Farley had been right: the girl did look good wet. Her delicate face, nude of makeup, looked appealingly young. A soaked silk dress molded her small pointed breasts and slight hips. Both she and her partner were barefoot, dripping seawater as Rex followed them cautiously below into a Berber-carpeted cabin with comfortable inbuilt bench seating and a fully equipped galley.

He located a pile of beach towels from a closet and opened the door to one of the staterooms so Sabine could get out of her wet dress. The man peeled off his T-shirt and waterlogged jeans. He was narrow in the shoulders, his dark hair a dramatic contrast to his face, which was still pinched and pale from the shock of jumping ship. Was he a rising star on the French stage or a server Sabine had met at a restaurant? Rex failed to see why she had chosen him over Brooklyn, but there were many things he still didn't know about the young woman.

"I didn't catch your name," he prompted, since it had not been volunteered.

"Jean-Luc. Valquez," the young man added with apparent reluctance. Thank you for saving us."

It speaks! Rex said to himself, reaching out to the breakfast bar to steady himself from the rolling motion of the sea. He heard urgent voices outside calling instructions to the sailboat.

Sabine stepped into the cabin, wrapped in a bright towel. "I will never get the tangles out of my hair," she said, tugging a comb through a damp strand. Under her only slight French accent lay the trace of a London one. Rex remembered she had lived, worked, and been schooled there.

"Perhaps you could rustle up a pot of coffee," he said, finding a packet of ground beans on a shelf. "It might help take your mind off your hair, and I'm sure we could all do with a cup." He took off the slicker and laid it over a chair.

"This is a nice yacht," she said, wandering into the galley, trailing her fingers over the granite breakfast bar. "It's like a mini-condo. Yours?"

"No, it belongs to a friend of Brook's"

"A Frenchman." Sabine waved the packet of French roast at him. "I remember now. An old salt by the name of Fabien."

"How did you get that cut on your wrist?" Rex asked while Jean-Luc watched on warily.

Rex watched the both of them, covertly, although neither seemed to pose a physical threat. And it was obvious the young man didn't want to get into any more trouble.

"I scraped it on some coral a few weeks ago while I

was diving," she replied, examining the long pink scar.

"Are you sure it wasn't self-inflicted?"

Slowly she filled the coffee maker with water. "What do you mean?" She stared at the machine, which began to burble and release a heady aroma of coffee.

"The strip torn from your white pareo, found at the promontory by the Plage d'Azur, has your blood on it. I suppose you cast the rest of it out to sea once you were aboard the catamaran, where Jean-Luc here was waiting for you with open arms."

The young man collapsed onto a stool at the counter and sank his head in his hands. "I helped her get away both times but that is all."

Sabine turned on him in a fury. "*Idiot!*" she said in French.

"Are you Sganarelle?"

Jean-Luc shrugged in submission. "It was her idea."

"*Veux-tu bien te taire, espèce de grenouille?*"

"Did she just call you a frog?" Rex asked.

Sabine smacked her forehead. "It's the first thing I thought of. I don't mean because he is French, but because he is a slimy little green reptilian thing with bony legs who won't shut up. *Cro-ak, cro-ak, cro-ak!*" she said in her boyfriend's face.

"*Ben, alors? Tu m'emmerdes avec tes histoires!*"

His rapid fire French left Rex none the wiser, but it sounded downright insulting. "How is the coffee coming along?" he asked brightly in an attempt to interrupt the domestic dispute.

The noise of engines and the motion of the yacht subsided. Rex looked out of a porthole and saw lilting crowns of palm fronds. They must be at anchor in the lee of an island. He hoped Pascal and Brooklyn were able to save the sailboat.

"Sganarelle was a code name," Rex told Sabine. "Taken from a play about a miserly and possessive old man—Vernon—and used for the pretend chiropractor, your lover."

She nodded slowly, a faint smile on her shapely lips. "How did you manage to figure that one out?" She plunked a mug of coffee and a container of sugar in front of him on the counter and poured another for herself and Jean-Luc.

"A friend of mine made the connection," Rex told her.

"Surely not the boring Windbag Winslow?"

"That's no way to speak about the man who took you in when you were a struggling young actress. Or is aspiring actress the proper term?"

"Oh, please. I paid rent and, anyway, it was Elizabeth's idea. I suppose you have no idea who she is, do you?" She raised a perfect eyebrow at him in defiance.

Rex drew a blank. "Other than being Paul Winslow's wife and co-owner of Swanmere Manor—"

"She's my mother! She got pregnant when she was an art student in Paris and gave me up at birth. I was adopted by a wealthy French couple and didn't find out I wasn't their biological daughter until Elizabeth breezed back in my life when I was eighteen. I have never forgiven my adoptive mother for not telling me herself. Nor Papa. As for my natural father, all I know is that he was a French actor and the love of Elizabeth's life, and a *salaud* for running out on her!"

Why had Paul Winslow not mentioned this important fact? It was another detail he had failed to disclose—like the fact Rex would be staying at a naturist resort. But perhaps Paul didn't know Sabine was his wife's daughter.

"Why did you marry Vernon if you didn't love him?" Rex asked the young actress. "Or did you once?"

"I thought he could take care of me."

"What happened when you went back there today?"

"Back where?"

"The maid Clementine saw you come out of your husband's cabana," Rex said. "Don't bother denying it."

Sabine remained silent and still for a moment, clearly stunned. Then she sighed. "You just can't trust anyone, can you? Even for one thousand euros..." She leaned back against the breakfast bar with her mug of coffee. "Vernon looked like he'd seen a ghost when I walked in." She gave a low laugh. "The expression on his face was priceless—usually he has such a poker face." She parodied his stony features. "He was in a maudlin mood, sitting in an armchairs listening to Broadway hits and knocking back the rum. I poured one for myself and launched into the role of Abjectly Sorry Wife."

"And you spiked his drink."

"He was pitiful when he realized what I'd done. We were in bed by then. 'What in hell did you put in my rum?'" she slurred in a perfect imitation of Vernon's dry American accent.

"'Barbiturates,' I told him. 'Everyone will think you topped yourself.'

"'Bitch. You planned this all along.' Then with his last gasp, he asked, 'Why?'

"'Because you asked for it.'"

Sabine paced the galley. "That's what he said when he slapped me at the Farley ranch in Texas: 'She asked for it.'" Hate transformed her exquisite face.

"There are other ways to get your husband out of your life, you know," Rex said.

"Not Vernon. Believe me, I tried. He didn't want to be twice divorced. Wouldn't look good on him. And he'd have killed my career dead. He was a very vindictive person."

Rex chose to overlook the hypocrisy of that last statement. "And you really thought you could get away with such an elaborate plan—down to the substitute clothes in the wardrobe?"

Sabine gave an elegant shrug of her shoulders. "Why not? The grieving husband drinks and medicates himself to death when the wife runs off with a younger man. Everyone would assume it was suicide because the door and glass sliders were locked. But I still had my key. By the time I resurfaced with my story of a desperate escape from a cruel husband, Vernon would already have been buried or cremated. I'd get all his money because we weren't divorced. And all the media attention would make me more bankable. I could have been offered a major movie deal. Now I may have to settle for someone else playing me in my own drama."

"I've always liked Angelina Jolie myself."

A flash of wry amusement illuminated Sabine's pale face. "Surely someone a bit younger and French?"

Jean-Luc snorted in derision from the other end of the breakfast bar. "You have no sense of reality, Sabine. You will get life in prison."

"My father is rich and will hire the best attorney, who will say it was self-defence."

"And you are claiming you had no knowledge of any of this?" Rex asked Jean-Luc.

"She said she had to leave her husband but was frightened of telling him. I had no idea she was going to kill him! She said she had to sneak back for something. I thought she meant some actual *thing* she had forgotten. *Quel cauchemar!*" His voice broke on the word "nightmare" and his face fell back into his hands.

"His speciality is drama," Sabine noted.

"He's an actor too?"

"We were in a stage adaptation of Daphne du Maurier's *Frenchman's Creek*, where he played the sensitive pirate Aubéry opposite my character, Dona St. Columb."

"A sensitive pirate?"

"It was a stupid play," Jean-Luc concurred.

"It was a success at the box office."

"Is that when you two met?" Rex asked.

A frozen silence ensued. He deduced he had touched on a nerve. At that moment, the churning vibration of the propellers started back up and the *Belle Dame* began to move.

Within twenty minutes, they were back in the bay preparing to embark in the dinghy with Pascal. The sailboat was already anchored and calmly cresting the waves, which had lost much of their furor. Brooklyn stood on shore, watching the four of them in the boat. Rex wondered what was passing through his mind as he waited for Sabine, and what sort of reception she would receive from the rest of the guests.

TWENTY

Brooklyn escorted the boat party to the main building, where Greg Hastings met them in the lobby and distributed white bathrobes embossed with La Plage d'Azur in gold on the breast pocket.

"Ms. Durand," he murmured, clearly not sure how to address his previous guest and murder suspect. He looked Jean-Luc over with polite curiosity before making a brief call from reception. "Lieutenant Latour is attending to a bad traffic accident," he informed Rex, 'but will be over just as soon as he can. Shall I inform the other guests of Ms. Durand's arrival? I don't think most of them are even aware she's alive. I instructed the staff to keep mum."

"Not yet," Rex said, reluctant to have the guests crowding in asking questions while he still had some of his own.

"What do you have to say for yourself?" Brooklyn finally asked Sabine.

"I don't have to answer to you."

The American threw up his arms in disbelief. "I

would have thought you have a lot of people to answer to. We all went looking for you. The police were here."

"Am I under arrest?" she asked Rex. "Can you make a citizen's arrest in a foreign country?"

"The Gendarmerie said to hold you for questioning," Hastings cut in politely. "In connection with your husband's death. I hope you understand."

"I had nothing to do with my husband's death."

"Ms. Durand," Rex objected. "You confessed on the yacht. Your plan, you said, was to resurface months later with your new beau and a watertight alibi, and claim your dead husband's estate."

"She probably hoped all the publicity would reignite her career," Brooklyn guessed correctly.

"What do you mean, 'reignite'?" Sabine asked defensively.

"You haven't been in anything lately."

"I have been resting. Mr. Graves put words in my mouth," she told the manager, appealing to him with her beguiling eyes. "I did not have my own lawyer present. The trauma of nearly drowning when our catamaran capsized..." She put a hand to her lovely throat, ever the consummate actress.

"My poor dear. Perhaps a snifter of brandy?"

"All round," Brooklyn suggested.

"Right." Hastings paced off in the direction of his office.

"Brook, you're soaked through," Rex said, watching him bundle himself in the white resort bathrobe.

"I swam out to the sinking sailboat on a rope. Pascal towed her into the bay. The owners, an older couple from Maine, offered us the use of their Saint Thomas villa whenever we like."

Sabine gazed at Brooklyn in overt admiration, perhaps thinking she would have had a better chance of escape with him. "You don't really think I murdered Vernon, do you, Brook?"

"Jean-Luc is a witness to your confession," Rex reminded her.

"I do not remember anything that was said, except that I had nothing to do with anything," the Frenchman said.

"Oh, so you do remember that much," Rex remarked.

"Take the young man to my office and keep an eye on him," Hastings instructed Winston, returning with the security guard and a cut-glass decanter. "I left a glass of brandy in there for you," he told Jean-Luc. "Make yourself comfortable. We'll accommodate Ms. Durand in the back office." The manager led her behind reception. Rex followed.

Sabine glanced around the functional space. "I need to call my father in Paris."

Minutes later, from outside the room, Rex could hear her agitated voice talking in French. "I'll go and see the guests now," he informed Hastings.

A throng of voices arose from the third cabana, occupied by the Winslows. Elizabeth was sobbing into a handkerchief on the sofa. "I must go to her," she cried.

Paul sat beside her, patting her hand. He looked up at Rex. "We saw you come back in the dinghy with Sabine. Thought we had all better sit tight and wait for you, though it was all I could do to prevent my wife from running out to the beach in the rain."

"Is it true Sabine had something to do with Vernon's death?" Dick Irving, the Canadian, asked from an armchair. "A maid saw her leave Vernon's cabana."

So much for keeping the guests in the dark. The turn in the weather had prompted them to wear a full set of clothes, no doubt a psychological reaction to the element of danger posed by the storm, and no doubt feeling uncomfortable and vulnerable being naked in front of the authorities.

"Ms. Durand acknowledges speaking with her husband," Rex confirmed.

"How is she?" Elizabeth asked, eyes red-rimmed from crying.

"She and her boyfriend had to abandon their catamaran, but they're both safe and dry now."

"I can't understand why she left a fortnight ago without saying goodbye." Elizabeth broke down again.

Toni Weeks gently pulled her from Paul's arms and assisted her to the bedroom. Glancing around the open-plan living room, Rex noticed the von Muellers installed at the kitchen table with Pam Farley and Nora O'Sullivan. A pot of tea and a half-demolished apple strudel stood on the pine surface.

"Would you like a cup?" Nora asked Rex. "You look blue."

"Thanks. It was a bit hairy out there."

"So brave of you to go out on the water in the storm."

"Daft," Sean corrected his wife.

"Where's Brook?" Duke Farley asked from the glass sliders overlooking the darkening windswept beach.

"I think he wanted to speak with Sabine alone."

"To think we'd all given her up for dead," Nora exclaimed.

"When can we see her?" Paul asked.

"I, for one, have no wish to see Sabine if she murdered her husband," Penny Irving said, filling the kettle.

The Texan pulled a cigar from his breast pocket. "Heck, I can't believe my racquet ball partner is lying dead in a morgue. Here's to you, buddy," he growled, knocking back a tumbler of amber liquor.

Rex addressed the Viennese doctor, who sat ponderously silent at table. "Ms. Durand said Vernon took a barbiturate with his rum."

Von Mueller tugged at his white beard thoughtfully. "*Ja*, a barbiturate taken with alcohol would have a compound effect, and in a large enough dose could cause death quickly. Especially a potent barbiturate like pentobarbital, used to euthanize animals. Or Thiopental, which is one of three drugs used in the United States to execute inmates."

"*Mein Gott!*" his wife exclaimed. "Max, you are scaring us!"

"I didn't find any drugs in the medicine cabinet next door," Rex assured her. Sabine must have brought the medication with her, and he now had an idea what.

Gaby was scribbling away in a notebook. "How does an overdose work, *Vater?*"

"It causes heart and respiratory failure. Then the person falls into a coma and can die."

"Would pentobarbital be used to treat horses?" Rex asked.

"For anesthesia *und* euthanasia, *ja*."

Yes, Rex concluded to himself: Sabine broke into the Sundown Ranch dispensary before she left for St. Barts, and perhaps Jean-Luc had been her accomplice. Hard to know how deep her leading man was implicated in all this. Perhaps he was just *acting* the part of a spineless twerp. David Weeks asked about the man she was with in the dinghy.

"He was her make-believe chiropractor," Rex explained. "There are clothes in her cabana that she purchased willy-nilly, sometimes in the wrong size, to explain away the extra time she was spending in Philipsburg. It was all a ruse to dupe her jealous husband. The man we brought in is in fact a French actor she worked with."

"Sabine always was a secretive one," Nora said from the table. "Not content with simply leaving Vernon, she wanted to taint him with scandal, even incriminate him in her suspected murder. But to be completely free of him, she had to finish him off." Murmurs of assent rose among the other guests. "It sends chills down my spine, it does, thinking how she planned it all."

"Gaby gave me the first real clue she was alive," Rex said. "She gets all the credit."

"So lucky we went to Saint Barts," the doctor agreed.

"And that Clementine from housekeeping saw her at the resort. Otherwise, by the time Sabine reentered public life, it might have been too late to prove she'd caused her husband's death." Rex set down his empty cup. "I should like to ask her a few more questions before the police take her into custody. I'll look in on Elizabeth on my way out."

This was the hard part. Confronting a mother's grief struck him as worse than facing a storm at sea.

TWENTY-ONE

Rex knocked on the bedroom door and, upon being invited in, found Elizabeth Winslow stretched out on the bed in conversation with Toni Weeks.

"I'll leave you to it," Toni said, slipping off the side of the bed.

Rex asked Elizabeth how she was feeling.

"Calmer now. Max prescribed a sedative."

"I thought perhaps you could take Sabine some clothes."

"Did she ask to see me?" Elizabeth asked hopefully. "I must look an absolute mess.'

The usually perfectly groomed Mrs. Winslow did look ravaged. "This must be so hard on you," Rex commiserated. "Sabine told me you were her mother. And now that I've met her I can see the resemblance." The greenish eyes, the hair color, though Elizabeth's was more red, her irises pure emerald.

"She's very beautiful, isn't she? Her father was the most handsome man I have ever met. It was a *coup de foudre*." Elizabeth's reminiscing sigh ended in a sob. "It's not been easy pretending to be just a friend all these years, but it's what she wanted. My parents forced me to give her up, but I never forgot her. On her eighteenth birthday, I returned to Switzerland to look for her. The director at the Maison de Lausanne was by now in a wheelchair and senile. The private clinic had reverted to a private house and she was taking in foreign students."

Elizabeth took a deep breath, as though drawing the stamina to continue. "An English girl studying French at the university said she'd seen piles of dusty boxes in the cellar, all alphabetized. It took us a while, and the cellar was dank and cold, but I was determined to find my baby!"

Fresh tears streamed down her face. Rex reached for the box of tissues by the bedside and placed it on her lap.

"Madame Bossard had kept meticulous records," Elizabeth said after composing herself. "I found my file and discovered that Sabine had been placed with a banker and his wife at a smart address in Paris."

"And that was your next destination," Rex prompted.

"Yes. I tracked Sabine down and told her everything. We met in a café on the boulevard Saint-Michel, and she said she'd always felt her mother couldn't be her real mum. They never got on. She was at a rebellious age, and our secret communications must have appealed to her creative imagination. Soon after, she came to London and got a job at David's restaurant, and I arranged for her to come and live at our house."

"And you confided in Paul?"

"Oh, yes. I told him about the adoption before we were married. We'd been married for ten years before I was reunited with my daughter. I never felt right about having other children. Paul has been so wonderfully supportive."

"That's why you were so keen for me to come to Saint Martin and help find out what happened to her. She was so much more than the friend you said she was."

"We felt the truth would have compromised the investigation. That you might think we were being over-protective. And Vernon, our prime suspect, was, in effect, our son-in-law, so it was all a bit awkward."

What a tangled web we weave, Rex thought. "Tell me about his phone."

"You know everything, don't you?" Elizabeth sat up straighter in bed. "Sabine said she needed information off it to help in divorcing him, but he always kept it in his safe. I went to her cabana the evening she went missing to give her a pair of earrings to wear to Paul's birthday. She wasn't there and Vernon was still out on his dive trip. I saw his phone lying around and took it, thinking I'd give it to Sabine later that evening. I still had it in my purse when we were out on the beach searching for her. It vibrated with an incoming call from the States. The security guards were approaching. I tried to switch it off. I didn't know what I'd do if they or the police searched us. I couldn't let Vernon know I had his phone. I panicked and chucked it onto the rocks. By that time I had a feeling something was terribly wrong, and I hoped the phone might point them to Vernon."

Rex thought how much simpler it might have been had he known the true relationship between Sabine and the Winslows, and about the phone. It would have given him more insight into Sabine's character. "You accidentally took a picture of yourself."

Elizabeth shook back her mass of red hair and pinned it up in a chignon. "I didn't know what I was doing. I was convinced Vernon had murdered Sabine. I wish to God she'd listened to me and not married him. Now her life is ruined and she'll be taken away from me again! They say what doesn't kill you makes you stronger. If I knew who 'they' were, I'd tell them to go to hell!"

"Well, I can tell you for a fact Sabine inherited some of her mother's character." Rex rubbed her shoulder in sympathy. "Are you ready to see her now?"

Elizabeth nodded and blew her nose. "I should go and splash cold water on my eyes," she said, scanning her face in a compact. "I don't want her to see me in this state. I'll pack a few things I had laundered for her. Does she have shoes?"

Rex shook his head. "No, and next door is a crime scene, so we won't be able to get in."

"We're close in shoe size. I can probably find her something of mine."

Paul Winslow stepped into the hall as they were leaving.

"I'm going with Rex to see Sabine," his wife told

him. "I wanted to slip out without the others knowing, so I could have some time alone with her."

"Send her my love." Paul took Elizabeth's face in his hands and kissed her forehead. "Chin up." He turned to Rex. "Don't be too hard on the girl."

Rex nodded in understanding. The Winslows had brought him out here to solve a mystery and he had accomplished his mission. The trouble was, it hadn't turned out the way they had expected. Yet from the moment he suspected Sabine was implicated in her husband's murder, he was morally bound to pursue the case to its bitter conclusion.

He opened the front door for Elizabeth. The rain had stopped, clearing the air and leaving the landscaped grass and tropical plants vibrantly fresh. He, by contrast, felt jaded and in need of a beer. They proceeded to the main building. A portable TV on the front desk showed pictures of a fatal pile-up outside Grand Case, caused by the earlier rainstorm. Pierre stood guard outside the small office, watching the news.

Rex explained his business and, leaving Elizabeth outside the door with a promise to be quick, went in to speak with Sabine. As soon as she saw him, she leaped from her straight-back chair. "Why do I have to stay confined in here?"

"It's too easy to disappear off this island."

"It wasn't when I tried earlier. Jean-Luc is such an imbecile. I hope his cell is more comfortable than mine." She indicated the small bare office with a brush of her slim hand. "But at least I was able to order room service."

"The officer in charge was called to a traffic emergency. I'm not sure how much longer you'll have to remain here. But an autopsy will be performed on your husband, and if a dangerous drug like pentobarbital is found in his system, you may well end up staying somewhere far worse—considering your connection to the ranch from where drugs were stolen."

Sabine tossed back her head in defiance. "I won't talk to the police. My father is hiring me the best lawyer."

"In the meantime I wondered if you could tell me what you know about Mr. Bijou."

"That cold fish? Why? What has he to do with this?"

"I'm looking into murders he may have committed."

She shivered in the bathrobe Hastings had brought her. "Are you referring to the two women who were found strangled on the island a few years ago?"

"And perhaps others in Amsterdam."

"I only met him a couple of times. A few weeks ago, he contacted me about doing some publicity for his Diamonds Are Forever Club in Marigot. I might have gone to see him but I had a prior engagement with Jean-Luc and was planning to leave the island."

"You're lucky. You may not have left the meeting alive. You're just his type."

"But the Gendarmerie issued a statement saying they had reason to believe the killer had left the island."

"It was baseless, as far as I was able to ascertain. I'd love to put an end to Bijou and his jewel fetishes before more women turn up dead. If you could give me something, anything, that might help in securing his conviction, you might get a lot of positive press. It might even help your case."

Sabine pouted prettily. "I don't want my name connected to his if he did what you say. But I can tell you this: He said I bore a striking resemblance to his mother, who abandoned him as a child. I looked into his eyes then and it was like staring through the gates of hell. I was fascinated and frightened at the same time. It would seem he hates his mother and wants to kill her over and over again."

"Aye, perhaps. Strangulation is personal. The jewels he leaves may be an ironic touch. She worked for a high-end escort service before she married his father, whom she left for another man."

Sabine collapsed in her chair. "I tried to get Vernon to buy a condo at his Marina del Mar. Of course, he was such a tightwad he wouldn't consider it."

"If Mr. Bijou is indeed a serial killer, it'll become known as Marina del Nightmare."

"You are quite funny. Vernon had no sense of humour."

"You don't have a lot of remorse, Sabine. A jury will want to see tears even if you plead self-defence."

"Don't worry, they will."

Rex had no doubt she would play to the jury. The story of her adoption would come out, and he wouldn't be surprised if Duke Farley appeared in court to testify to Vernon's physical abuse of her at his Silver Springs Ranch. Her biological mother would make an impassioned plea for leniency. "I'll leave you with your mother now," Rex said and called Elizabeth into the office.

"Mummy!" Sabine cried, throwing herself into Mrs. Winslow's arms.

"My darling child," Elizabeth said, stroking her daughter's long copper-colored hair. "What have you done!?"

TWENTY-TWO

Standing outside Greg Hastings' office, Lieutenant Latour fondled his mustache with smug satisfaction. "You see, I was right about Mademoiselle Durand not being dead."

"You said she was eaten by sharks," Rex reminded him, returning his waterproof cape.

"But not murdered, *monsieur*. Ze alleged murder victim turned out to be ze murderer."

Paul Winslow gave a heartfelt sigh. "It's been hard on Elizabeth, first thinking her daughter was dead, then finding out she was alive, only to have her arrested for murdering her husband."

"You should look into Mr. Bijou again," Rex entreated the gendarme.

Latour, who already carried heavy purple bags under his eyes, contrived to look even more exhausted. "On what pretext?"

"He may well be the Amsterdam Jewel Killer. He faced charges there for murdering women in the same manner as the two here on Saint Martin. It would be a feather in your kepi to bring him to justice."

"If I live to see it. Monsieur Bijou has many loyal persons working for him."

"Well, you can't have him running the island. One of the victims was found across the border on Sint Maarten. Even if you don't have the balls here to bring Bijou to justice, at least cooperate with the Dutch authorities."

"Ze balls? What are ze balls we do not have?" Latour asked in all innocence.

Rex moved on quickly. "I can give you his profile, from when he was Coenraad van Bijhooven, compiled by Interpol." A slight exaggeration, but it caught the lieutenant's interest. "It details all his nefarious activities in Amsterdam,"

Latour stood to attention. "Very well. Leave it to me, *monsieur*."

"God help us," Winslow muttered behind Rex's shoulder. "D'you think it'll do much good?" he asked when the lieutenant stepped aside to take a call on his cell phone.

"At the very least, it'll make Bijou feel extremely uncomfortable when it all gets out. People won't be so willing to hand over their money to him."

"He may just skip town."

"He can't run forever."

"*Marigot*?" Latour asked sharply on his phone. "*Mais non, voyons, c'est impossible! Mademoiselle Durand est ici sous surveillance.*"

Rex and Winslow exchanged puzzled looks. How could Sabine be in Marigot? Latour stormed through the lobby, his mustache set in a rigid line.

"Has she escaped?" Rex asked, rushing after him. He had left her with her mother not twenty minutes ago, or however long it had taken him to go back to his cabana to shower and change.

Pierre was still at his post watching the news. Latour signaled to him to open the door to the small office. Sabine looked up from the desk where she was writing a note, her mother sitting close by.

Latour turned on his heels. "It is not to be believed. Ze police in Marigot informed me Mademoiselle Durand was found dead. Zey did not know we had her. Someone fitting her description was discovered in an abandoned farmhouse, dead for a couple of weeks, it appears."

"Who is it then?" Winslow asked.

"Another of Bijou's victims," Rex suggested.

"Ze builder for ze renovation, he goes in to check for flooding after all zis heavy rain. He looks in ze cellar. Ah, ze scene zat meets his eyes and nose sickens him, and he calls the emergency services."

"Was there a gem in the woman's navel?"

"*Eh, oui*. A small dark red stone. *Un grenat*."

"A garnet," Winslow translated.

"Before she dies, she is able to write B-I-J on ze cellar floor with her blood." Latour donned his cap. "I will take Mademoiselle Durand and Monsieur Valquez to ze police station and then assist in ze arrest of zis monster. *Salut, messieurs!*"

As Sabine was escorted from the main building, she slipped an envelope into Rex's hand. He watched while Latour and his sergeant installed her and her wretched-looking boyfriend in the police car, and then set foot toward his cabana.

Brooklyn sat on the patio staring out to where the yellow umbrellas flopped one by one as the beach attendant shut the concession down for the night. There had not been many takers, even after the sun made a brief and reluctant appearance that afternoon. The Irvings, undeterred, were practicing yoga positions in perfect sync on the sand.

"I'm not really one for this naturist culture," Rex confided in his roommate.

Brooklyn shrugged with a smile. "To each his own."

"Sabine gave me this." Rex deposited the envelope on the table. "It's addressed to you."

Brooklyn gazed at it for a long moment before breaking the seal. Rex went back inside for two beers. When he returned, the note lay in a crumple ball on the table. He sat down.

"Brook, I wanted to ask about that woman from Philipsburg you were dating two years ago."

"Gerry Linder."

"You just answered my question." So it *was* Geraldine Linder, the murdered tour guide in Thad's report. When Brooklyn had referred to her as "Gerry," Rex had not immediately made the connection. "A new body has just come to light—similar M.O."

"Body?"

"I'm afraid Gerry was one of two women murdered on the island two years ago. That we know about."

Brooklyn looked flummoxed. "I didn't know. After I found out about her involvement with Bijou and ended our relationship, I went round to her apartment. I was flying back to the States the next day and thought I'd say goodbye. You know—no hard feelings. Her landlady said she'd left suddenly and two men had been in and cleaned her place out."

Bijou's men, no doubt. "She was found in August, missing since the end of July."

"I was back home August first and must've missed the story."

"It was quickly quashed to protect Bijou."

"You think he had something to do with it?" Brooklyn asked in surprise.

"I think he had everything to do with it."

The American nodded slowly. "So that's why you went to The Stiletto."

"I went there to see if he had an alibi for the night Sabine went missing. He did. But it seems he had designs on her too."

"We must have similar taste in women." Brooklyn reached for the crumpled paper ball and cupped his hand over it—protectively, as Rex thought. "What's going to happen now?"

"It's out of my hands. I came to solve the mystery of Sabine Durand. But we can inform the Gendarmerie about Gerry's connection to Mr. Bijou, which was previously unknown. Sean will be happy to hear he was right about him. To be honest, I thought at first our Irish friend's theories were pure flights of fancy." Rex stretched expansively in his chair. "My stay here has been an interesting experience in so many ways." But now he was ready to go home.

"D'you think you'll ever return to Saint Martin?" the American asked.

"Who knows? Will you?"

Brooklyn gave a shrug and flicked the ball of paper off the table.

The resort guests would migrate back to their countries of origin, perhaps to return next summer, but the prize butterfly would no longer be among them. Sabine Durand would grace the gray cell of a prison for many years to come.

"So—looks like you've been busy, Rex. And not just with murder cases." Brooklyn raised an eyebrow in a quizzical expression. "David said you had a woman visitor while I was away. I'm assuming it wasn't that social worker in Iraq?"

"No. Her name is Helen."

"A girl in every port, huh?"

Rex coughed modestly. "Just one."

"Hope it all works out for you, buddy."

"I have a feeling it will—but you never know what life will throw at you, do you?"

"You just gotta play it for all it's worth." Brooklyn raised his bottle in a toast.

"Here's to that," Rex said, saluting him with his Guinness.

REX GRAVES MYSTERY TITLES

Christmas Is Murder
Murder on St. Martin
Murder on the Moor
Murder of the Bride
Murder at the Dolphin Inn
Murder at Midnight
Murder Comes Calling
Judgment of Murder
Upstaged by Murder

Shorter Rex Graves Mystery Titles:
Prelude to Murder
Say Murder With Flowers
Say Goodbye to Archie

PRAISE FOR THE REX GRAVES MYSTERY SERIES

Christmas Is Murder (*starred review*)
"The first installment in this new mystery series is a winner... A must for cozy fans." ~*Booklist*

"Challinor will keep most readers guessing as she cleverly spreads suspicion and clues that point in one direction, then another." ~*Alfred Hitchcock Mystery Magazine*

Murder on St. Martin
"...the plot twists are worthy of Erle Stanley Gardner." ~*Booklist*

Murder on the Moor
"The past intrudes when the acquittal of a suspected child murderer brings back memories of the Moor Murders case, and later when an old flame of Rex's turns up on the doorstep. Challinor skillfully choreographs all." ~*The Washington Post*

"This is a nice series, with a bonnie flavor of Scotland."

~*Deadly Pleasures*

Murder of the Bride
"The setting, an English country home, is as much a character as the people, and many of those characters are a delight." ~*Buried Under Books*

Murder at the Dolphin Inn
"With numerous plots and twists, *Murder at the Dolphin Inn* provides a first class whodunit." ~Cozy *Mystery Book Reviews*

Murder at Midnight
"What could be better for Agatha Christie whodunit fans than an old-fashioned, Scottish country house murder on New Year's Eve?" ~*Mystery Scene*

"This is a classic country-house mystery, with modern day twists and turns adding to the fun." ~*Booklist*

Murder Comes Calling
"Smooth prose will keep cozy fans turning the pages." ~*Publishers Weekly*

"This seventh in the series nicely mixes procedural detail and village charm and will appeal to fans of Deborah Crombie and Anne Cleeland." ~*Booklist*

Judgment of Murder
"Intriguing... Readers will eagerly await Rex's further adventures." ~*Publishers Weekly*

"Multiple plotlines, a long-distance romantic relationship, and a cast of interesting, well-drawn characters add to this satisfying mystery." ~*Booklist*

Upstaged by Murder
"Fans–and there are many–will be shouting 'Bravo!" ~*Booklist*

"Challinor takes the further step of recruiting the stars of those classic novels to help solve the case." ~*Kirkus Reviews*

THE AUTHOR

Now living in Southwest Florida, C.S. Challinor was raised and educated in Scotland and England, and holds a joint honours degree from the University of Kent, Canterbury, as well as a minor in psychology. She is a member of the Authors Guild. Her author website is www.rexgraves.com.

She has made two trips to St. Martin, touring the Caribbean island north and south, and stayed on the French side, where there was a naturist resort on beautiful Orient Beach.

Printed in Great Britain
by Amazon

83997079R00129